Pam's behavior this morning was proof enough to Leah's mind that Kay was wrong about the southern girl. Now all Leah had to do was get Kay to admit it.

"Kay," Leah started, "about Pam—" Leah paused to pick up her right toe shoe. She wrapped a small padding of lambswool around the ends of her toes and wriggled her foot into the satin slipper. "I think you're—eek!"

Leah's shriek echoed throughout the studio. Leah kicked her foot, and her new toe shoe went sailing through the air, landing in the middle of the room with a thud. Something gray and fuzzy rolled out.

"Ooh!" Linda yelled, jumping out of the way of the round gray object. "What is it?"

"A mouse!" Katrina pronounced. "It's dead."

"Stephenson, what is the meaning of this?" Madame's stern voice broke through the chorus of scared voices and cries of disgust.

The SATIN SLIPPERS Series
by Elizabeth Bernard
Published by Fawcett Girls Only Books:

TO BE A DANCER (#1)

CENTER STAGE (#2)

STARS IN HER EYES (#3)

CHANGING PARTNERS (#4)

SECOND BEST (#5)

Other titles in the Girls Only series available upon request

CURTAIN CALL

Satin Slippers #6

Elizabeth Bernard

FAWCETT GIRLS ONLY • NEW YORK

RLI: $\dfrac{\text{VL 7 \& up}}{\text{IL 8 \& up}}$

A Fawcett Girls Only Book
Published by Ballantine Books
Copyright © 1988 by Cloverdale Press, Inc.

Library of Congress Catalog Card Number 87-92126

ISBN 0-449-13309-5

Manufactured in the United States of America

First Edition: August 1988

Special thanks to Capezio by Balletmakers, and Danskin.

For Richard, who partnered me through

Chapter 1

"Robson's a real Dr. Jekyll and Mr. Hyde," Pamela Hunter complained as she joined Leah Stephenson in a corner of the San Francisco Ballet Academy's third floor rehearsal studio. Leah agreed with Pam, but she was afraid to nod her head or say anything out loud. Christopher Robson, who was coaching this practice session for the upcoming student performance of *Swan Lake*, had his pale blue eyes focused right on Leah and Pam.

"Hunter," he ordered in a soft but serious voice, "we'll skip to your first variation—"

"Again?" the redhead protested.

"And again, and again, and again!" Mr. Robson's voice rose, and his faint British accent grew more pronounced. "We will keep repeating it until you begin to look like you are dancing it."

With a sulky sigh Pam stepped in front of Leah and squeezed her strongly arched feet into fifth position. Mr. Robson rapped a metal yardstick against the wooden seat of a high stool that stood in the front of the small, overheated room. "And one, and two, and three," he counted. The accompanist, Robert Lipman, nodded in Pam's direction to cue her for her entrance. Leah thought she detected a flicker of pity on Robert's face. Leah knew Robert was not crazy about Pamela Hunter— not many people at SFBA were. But Robert had a soft heart, and he could tell that Robson was picking on Pam.

Pam sprang onto pointe so hard that Leah's toes ached in sympathy. Then she thudded across the studio floor in a series of hard little hops. Pam was strong and sturdy and had feet with muscles hard as steel: she scorned padding the inside of her shoes with bits of cotton or lambswool. She didn't need to: the toes of her tights were never bloody after pointe class, unlike most of the other girls. Still, Leah sensed that if Pam kept dancing so violently, she was going to get hurt. Leah pressed her back against the wooden barre that ran around three walls of the mirrored room. The December sun shined through the tall dirty windows of the Victorian mansion, streaking Leah's upswept blond hair gold; the rays illuminated the crystal teardrops of the old-fashioned chandelier, throwing rainbows of color down at Pamela's feet. The effect was oddly magical and completely at odds with Pam's interpretation of the dainty footwork. Leah folded her arms across her chest and slowly shook her head. Pam's performance reminded her of something. After a moment Leah finally remembered it was something Andrei Levintoff had told her.

Andrei was a guest artist with the Bay Area Ballet Company and occasionally taught at SFBA. Less than a month ago he had lectured Leah about attacking steps, accusing her of dancing as if she wanted to hurt someone—possibly herself. During practice for the Louise Adams Scholarship competition Leah had driven herself harder than ever before, dancing with the kind of fury Pam danced with now. Leah wasn't exactly angry then, but she had been afraid that she didn't have the right stuff for a top-notch ballet career. One night while rehearsing, Andrei had told Leah she was dancing just like Pam. He had said that he felt sorry for Pamela Hunter: she had the makings of a great dancer, but he had a feeling she hated to dance more than anything else in the world.

Looking at Pam now, Leah knew Andrei had been right. Pam really did seem to despise dancing. Why was she going through all this torture, then? Leah regarded Pam more carefully. The attractive redhead was continuing to stamp her way through the delicate pointe work. Every expressive movement of her athletic body betrayed her anger. With each pirouette, Pam used Christopher's face as her point of focus and paused just long enough to glare at him. The slightly built man was now perched on the wooden stool with one leg drawn up and his strongly defined chin propped on his knee. He watched Pam carefully through his glasses, his eyes expressionless, although Leah could imagine what he was thinking: Pam was purposely flaunting her terrible rendition of the variation in his face. And as dreadfully as Pamela was dancing just then, Leah had to admire her rebellious performance. She only wished she had half the guts Pamela Hunter did, at least when it came to dealing with Christopher Robson.

The retired British-born dancer was the one teacher at the prestigious dance school that Leah loathed. Until rehearsals had started for the all-student performance of *Swan Lake*, Leah hadn't studied with him very much. But in the two short weeks of his coaching sessions, he had almost completely demoralized Leah. In spite of his charmingly boyish good looks, the gray-haired Christopher—or Mr. Robson, as he insisted on being called—was a real ogre in the classroom. He seemed to believe a generous dose of sarcasm, peppered with cruel, cutting remarks of the most personal nature, would inspire his dancers to reach for the stars. His effect on Leah had been quite the opposite. Usually she left one of Robson's rehearsals more inspired to hang up her toe shoes for good than ever to dance again. She usually felt like burning her tutus and running down to the bus station to catch the first bus back to her hometown of San Lorenzo, California.

Just then Christopher jumped down from the stool. He tapped his metal yardstick against his thigh as his pale eyes followed Pam's progress through three more steps of the enchaînement. Without warning he threw the ruler down, and it skidded across the smooth floor, landing just inches short of Pam's feet.

"*Stop!*" Christopher yelled. Pam jerked to a halt and Robert ended with a dissonant chord. Christopher winced at the sound.

"Sorry," Robert murmured.

Pam drew in a sharp angry breath and planted her hands on her hips. She turned to face Christopher and boldly met his cold gaze. Brusquely she rubbed the sweat off her forehead with the back of her hand.

Next to Leah, Kenny Rotolo let out a quiet whistle. "Old Faithful's about to blow!" he commented in a hushed voice.

Apparently Kenny's whisper wasn't quite soft enough. Christopher whirled around, and his eyes came to rest on Leah. In a cool voice he asked with exaggerated politeness, "Miss Stephenson, please, I'd be delighted if you'd share your comments with the rest of us."

Leah looked at the teacher with frightened blue eyes. "Uh—I didn't say anything, Mr. Robson," she managed to get out, angry at herself for stammering.

He arched his eyebrows, then looked up at the ceiling. Leah held her breath. So far today she'd been spared Christopher's criticism. For a moment she thought her luck had run out. But apparently Christopher didn't think Leah was worth his attention this particular afternoon. Slowly and with great deliberation he turned toward Pam.

"As for you, Miss Hunter. I *have* seen unmusical dancing in my time. I *have* seen more than my share of clumsy young women take up precious space in the classroom. I *have* seen all sorts of unpleasant renditions of classical ballet both in classrooms and on stage. But I must congratulate you." He paused and applauded Pam silently. "I have never seen anyone dance more like a well-trained circus elephant than you."

An angry blush crept up Pam's neck and onto her face. Smiling, Mr. Robson approached Pam, not taking his eyes off her face. A foot or so from her he stopped, then bent down gracefully to pick up his yardstick. Without missing a beat he concluded, "In fact, I will definitely keep you in mind should I hear that anyone is looking to cast the ballet version of *Dumbo*! Your performance just now would certainly guarantee you the lead!"

Leah's mouth fell open in horror. Behind her someone gasped. The most humiliating thing that could happen to a girl in an Academy classroom was to be told she was fat. And Pam was definitely *not* fat. She was well-built, solid, and weighed more than other girls her height, but she still looked slender.

But Pam was an expert at not letting Robson get to her. Except for the color on her high-boned cheeks, Pam weathered Mr. Robson's sarcastic outburst with remarkable calmness.

"Why Mr. Robson!" Pam protested. "I was just doing what you told me to do." She opened her large green eyes very wide and looked completely innocent. "You said to emphasize each step, give it character. I do believe 'emphasize' was the exact word you used." Pam turned around and winked at Leah. Leah flashed Pam a warning look. Didn't Pam realize Robson could see her face in the mirror? Pam must really be enjoying her fight with Christopher, Leah thought.

From the opposite corner someone stifled a nervous giggle.

Mr. Robson pounded his yardstick on the floor, and the room instantly became silent. All Leah could hear was the clanging noise that the steam pipes made and the nervous beating of her own heart. He eyed each of the nine dancers in the cramped studio in turn. In a slow, deliberate voice he said, "We will now take it from the top again. Second and third cast, please dance full out this time. No marking!"

Everyone groaned. But Christopher Robson seemed not to hear. He strolled back to the black baby grand and gave Robert the signal to begin. Three sets of dancers lined up. Leah, Pam, and Kenny were the first cast. They were lucky: they'd have the most space to dance in. Behind Leah, Abigail Handhardt gave a little shove. "Move up, Stephenson, you're stepping on me."

Leah wasn't stepping on Abby, but she obligingly led her line of dancers a foot or so forward. Leah didn't want to start an argument with anyone. Everyone was acting tired and cranky. Rehearsal was running so late, Leah was sure she, Linda, and Suzanne were going to miss dinner back at Mrs. Hanson's house. Leah had grabbed only an apple for lunch, and she barely had the energy to mark the pas de trois again, let alone dance it full out. Making them all go through the entire routine again was crazy: everyone was exhausted. Someone is going to get hurt if Christopher doesn't stop soon, Leah thought, putting one well-pointed foot behind her and drawing herself up into her opening position.

When the music started, Leah counted six beats then led Kenny and Pam across the floor, being sure to stop at a piece of masking tape that marked the spot for her first turn. Out of the corner of her eye Leah checked the mirror to be sure she and Pam were in a straight line, then, wearing her best ballerina smile, she executed a double pirouette. The turn was so centered, she was able to pause for the briefest of instants at the end of it before hopping off pointe and going into her preparation for the next enchaînement. The stiff, forced smile on her face gave way to a genuine grin. For the first time that afternoon, dancing actually felt good, as if it came naturally to Leah. Maybe she was wrong about Robson. Maybe he really knew what he was doing.

"Stephenson!" Christopher screamed, loud enough to be heard over the music. A split second later Robert stopped playing and Leah faced the front of the room, truly confused.

The teacher put his hands on his hips and tapped his foot angrily against the floorboards. "Show me which is your right hand and which is your left!" he said to Leah.

"My what?" Leah asked, not quite sure she'd heard right.

Christopher reached out with his ruler and lightly rapped Leah's wrist. "Is this your left or right hand?" he asked.

Leah snatched her hands away and hid them behind her back. She took a couple of quick steps backward and somehow treaded on Pam's toe. "Sorry!" she murmured.

Pam gave Leah's arm a reassuring squeeze. "Pretend you don't know," she whispered. Pam put her hand in the small of Leah's back and shoved her forward a little.

His eyes dared her to answer wrong, and for a moment Leah considered taking Pam's advice. But she didn't have the nerve. She raised her hand and said in an embarrassed voice, "This is my right hand."

"Correct. I'm surprised you can tell. You had me fooled!" Mr. Robson retorted. "We have danced this piece at least ten times today, and probably a hundred times since we started rehearsals. You will dance it a hundred more times before next

Thursday's performance *if* I decide you are good enough to actually appear in that performance. But any student above the elementary level in a school of this caliber who still doesn't know which direction they're turning in certainly isn't ready for even a walk-on role in a staged production!" he yelled.

As he talked, Leah mentally reviewed the passage she had just danced. "I turned the wrong way!" she said to herself as she kicked the toe of her shoe hard against the floor.

Instantly Christopher mimicked her California accent. "I turned the wrong way!" He shook his head in amazement. "The guy who invented the term 'dumb blonde' must have met you somewhere along the line."

Leah's bottom lip trembled. Christopher didn't need to put her down just for turning the wrong direction. Lots of good dancers got their turns all mixed up. It was a common mistake. Madame Preston generally corrected Leah with a laugh whenever she pirouetted the wrong way. But Christopher had to make her look like an idiot in front of everyone, just like he did every day during rehearsal. For two weeks Leah had managed not to cry in front of him. Except for Pam, she was the only girl present who had not. But Leah definitely felt as if she was about to cry now—maybe because today's practice was running later than usual, and her whole body ached to be back at the boardinghouse soaking in a tub of hot water and bath salts, or maybe because her tolerance for Christopher's caustic tongue had simply run out.

Leah turned her back on Christopher, pulled a

couple of hairpins from her bun, and tucked them back in again. She tugged at her leotard and marched back to her starting position as Christopher motioned for Robert to start the music again. "Pick it up from where you left off, glissade, assemblé over, et cetera," he called crisply over her shoulder.

One tear spilled out of Leah's blue eyes, then another as she returned to the small piece of masking tape on the floor. She wiped the sleeve of her old blue leotard across her face. Suddenly Pamela was behind Leah. "Don't give him the satisfaction," Pam whispered. "Miss Charlotte, my teacher back home, said Pavlova couldn't tell her right from her left either. So there." Leah had a feeling Pamela had just made that up, but it made her feel better anyway. She dabbed at one last tear as Pam went on. "And speaking of dumb, it's a good thing he didn't go in for acting!" she commented. "He certainly can't do impressions of ballerinas."

Leah looked up at Pam, who was grinning. The redhead had an evil-looking glint in her green eyes. She scurried past Leah, winked, then put her feet and arms in fifth position and said. "He made you sound like you came from Brooklyn— not California!"

For some reason that struck Leah as funny, and she had to suppress a giggle. Kenny caught Leah's eye and started to chuckle.

The music began again. Leah forced herself to keep a straight face and opened her arms in a broad, expansive second position. She made a mental note to thank Pam later. Though the two girls had been anything but friends until now,

Leah was really beginning to appreciate the feisty redhead. Having her as a partner in this pas de trois sure helped weather the storm called Christopher Robson.

Leah lilted her way through the next combination of steps, holding her breath the whole time, just waiting for Christopher to criticize her again. She stepped into a graceful attitude turn that ended that segment of the pas de trois, held her position, then ran behind another strip of masking tape into what would be the opposite wing onstage. Leah grabbed a towel off the barre and dabbed at her sweaty face. While she caught her breath she watched Kenny and Pam dancing the short pas de deux that ended the first part of the piece. Pam had stopped her angry display, and she was dancing more like herself.

Leah admired Pamela's strength and technique. What she lacked in interpretation, she more than made up for with strong personal charisma and a flashy style. Leah had a feeling that Pamela Hunter would someday go far in the dance world: she was beautiful in a dramatic way and had the knack of drawing attention to herself. Leah hoped when the time came to audition for companies that she wouldn't be in the same room with Pam. Even in a dingy classroom the flamboyant redhead had the air of being larger than life. Next to her, blond, blue-eyed, and small-boned Leah often felt as if she faded right into the woodwork.

Leah couldn't quite believe how her feelings toward Pam had changed lately. She knew it had something to do with these awful daily sessions with Mr. Robson. Pam had shown a different side of herself, standing up to the mean-spirited teacher.

She never minced words when he was harsh or unfair to her. And if she didn't exactly stand up for the other students, she had a way of supporting them with her comments when Robson wasn't looking. Leah was beginning to suspect Pamela Hunter wasn't all that bad—and that was an opinion that truly surprised her.

Back in September, Pam had singled Leah out as the girl to beat at the auditions for the Academy. Pam had played a dirty trick on Leah by performing the same variation, and Leah had never wanted to see Pam—never mind talk to her—again. But both of them had been accepted to the Academy. Relations between the two had been terrible until now. For the first month at SFBA Leah and Pam had barely exchanged a word, though they lived in the same boardinghouse a few blocks from the school. And when the cast list for *Swan Lake* had been posted, Leah had nearly died. Leah, Kenny, and Pam were slated to dance the pas de trois in the first act. Besides second and fourth act corps work, she and Pam were also listed to dance the mazurka in the third act ballroom scene. The prospect of working so closely day after day with Pam seemed to be some kind of cruel punishment, especially coming right on the heels of Leah's disappointment in not winning the Louise Adams Scholarship and losing the lead role of Odette/Odile to Katrina Gray.

But as Madame Preston always said, working side by side in a dance studio with someone could teach you more about her in two weeks than you'd learn in ten years of ordinary social contact. Madame sure was right as far as Pam was concerned. Leah didn't exactly consider Pam a friend these days. She was too wary of Pam for that. But she was grateful for Pam's support as far as Christopher was concerned, and Leah had grown to respect Pam's dedication, hard work, and willingness to throw herself into a role. Pam's fighting spirit had kept the rehearsals going when everyone was ready to quit. And Leah appreciated her for that, because in one very important way, Leah had finally accepted she was just like Pam: she wanted more than anything in the world to become a great ballerina, and the only way to make her dream come true was not to let the Christophers of the ballet world get to her.

Chapter 2

"*Wake up, Stephenson!*" *Christopher's* voice startled Leah out of her daydream. "You're on the wrong side for your next entrance. You should have crossed behind the backdrop right after your exit." Leah blushed and scurried behind Pam as the redhead began her quick exiting series of jetés.

Before Pam's music ended, the studio door flew open, and a small crowd of dancers trooped in. In the lead was Andrei Levintoff, an energetic young man with unruly blondish-brown hair and deepset blue eyes. Behind him, Leah spotted all her good friends: Katrina Gray, Alexandra Sorokin, Finola Darling, and Kay Larkin. They were still in their practice clothes, though from the soda can in Finola's hand, Leah suspected they had just tramped up the back stairs from the cafeteria.

Behind Kay the door swung shut with a loud bang, and the petite dark-haired girl let out a high-pitched giggle. Robert stopped his music and looked expectantly from Christopher to the door, as if not quite sure what to do next.

"Andrei?" Christopher addressed the young man with a frown. "We're still rehearsing."

Andrei half shrugged, half smiled at the teacher. It wasn't a very apologetic gesture, and Christopher's frown deepened. Andrei searched the room. His eyes lit on Leah, and he smiled. Turning to Christopher, Andrei said in his thick Russian accent, "Sorry. I do not mean to interrupt your rehearsal, but it is late and I thought you finish by now. Madame wanted me to give these to people before they go home. I can now. Or I leave them with you until after you finish?" He waved a stack of magazines in the air for Christopher to see.

The perpetual frown on the older man's forehead deepened, but he gave an offhand shrug, as if he really didn't care, and said, "There is no point in going on today. We are getting nowhere anyway. You can go now." He waved his hand at the class, and the whole room sighed with relief. After a brief pause the students acknowledged their teacher with a short round of halfhearted applause.

The powerfully built young danseur strode across the room toward Leah. "What is it, Andrei?" she asked, wiping the sweat off her chest and back with a towel. Alexandra hurried close on Andrei's heels and grinned at Leah over his shoulder. The rest of Leah's friends crowded around, and Kay looked as if she were bursting with some kind of incredible news. Too tired to be excited, Leah walked over to her dance bag, where she pulled out an old pair of lilac leg warmers and a blue sweater.

"Wait until you see, Leah!" Kay bubbled, her dark short-cropped curls bobbing as she talked. Finola clapped her hand over Kay's mouth.

"Love, it's not your place to tell Leah. It's Andrei's big news," she scolded in a crisp British accent. Finola was this year's exchange student from the Royal Ballet School in London and had arrived in SFBA only a few weeks before.

Leah shrugged on her sweater and massaged her right calf gingerly. "What's going on?" she asked.

"This is the new *FootNotes*." Andrei placed a copy of the slick dance magazine in Leah's hand. Everyone here gets one," he told the other dancers, who were hanging around trying to figure out exactly what was going on.

His announcement was greeted with a chorus of oohs and ahhs, and a forest of hands reached up toward the stack Andrei held slightly out of reach and above his head. Pam jumped up and secured the first copy with her brightly painted fingernails. Andrei frowned at her but continued to distribute magazines as he talked. "This has the story about the Academy. You remember the reporter and photographer were here last month?"

Pam let out a triumphant little laugh. "Now, this will be something to write home about!" she predicted, turning page after page of the glossy journal. "Where is it? Don't tell me they buried the feature back in the classified ads!" she grumbled.

Leah found the article first. "Oh, it's beautiful!" she cried. "Andrei, where did you get all these advance copies?"

Andrei tapped the magazine with his finger. "Look. You must look, not talk. This is wonderful, Leah. It is very good for you."

Katrina sidled up next to Leah to see better.

Kenny craned his neck and peered over Katrina's head.

"Turn the page, Leah, turn the page," Alexandra urged. Leah ran her finger down the first column and quickly scanned the description of the school. "Look at this great shot," she mumbled. Her eyes lingered on the picture of the renovated old mansion and the insets showing the modern additions to the art studio, the swimming pool, and the dilapidated but still lovely greenhouse. "They gave us so much space in here," she said happily, looking right up at Andrei. "This is really great." Kay reached over Leah's shoulder and turned the next page. Leah had to blink twice to make sure she wasn't seeing things. "I don't believe it!" she shrieked.

"I do," Pam said in a dry voice. She tossed her copy of the magazine on the floor. "Teacher's pet is always teacher's pet. It really pays off in the end, doesn't it?" Her voice was bitter, and she quickly pushed her way out of the eager crowd of students.

Leah didn't think much about it—she was used to Pam's jealous accusations. Besides, she was still staring at the glossy two-page spread. Leah was shown on pointe in a filmy wisp of a costume, leaning into a deep backbend with her arms around Andrei's neck. The moody black and white photo captured her favorite moment from *Circles*, a one-act modern ballet Andrei had choreographed on Leah for the annual Academy fund-raising gala. It was a flattering picture: Leah's thick blond hair hung freely below her waist, her profile was lovely, and the angle of the shot made her already pretty eyes look spectacular. The way Andrei was looking at Leah in the picture made her blush.

"Oh, Andrei, did you know about this ahead of time? That this picture would have so much space?" she cried, keeping her eyes on the picture. Seeing it brought back all the confusing feelings she had had for the handsome Russian dancer. She was pretty sure she was over her crush by now, but the photo had captured a moment that had felt very special and private— even if it was a stage moment and make-believe romance.

"No. I do not know until today. Madame call me to the office to say this group of magazines for you—I mean me—" The recent émigré looked terribly confused.

"You mean," Alex said with a throaty laugh, "she told you these copies were personally yours." Alex had known Andrei since their childhood in Leningrad together, and she usually knew what he was trying to say.

Andrei nodded, grateful for Alex's help, and smiled warmly at Leah. Leah couldn't help but grin back. All of a sudden she noticed how quiet the room had become.

Apparently Andrei noticed it, too. "But it is not just Leah who looks wonderful," he said. Leah decided that if Andrei Levintoff hadn't been a dancer, he would have made a great diplomat. She felt a little embarrassed that the photo of her and Andrei was splashed across half the article, while a quick glance down the page revealed that the other girls were all in group shots that made them look like students, not stars.

"No," Abigail whined, "but Leah got to dance with you, so she gets all the publicity."

Finola traded glances with Leah and quickly spoke up. "You mean," she said, batting Andrei's arm lightly, "*Mr. Levintoff* got all the publicity! You know how hot the press gets about a new defector from the USSR. How well he dances doesn't even matter," Finola teased.

Everyone started laughing, including Andrei, and the subtle tension Leah felt a moment before disappeared. Leah inwardly thanked Finola. Finola hadn't been around long, but she had already become very popular at the school. She was shrewd about people and even more diplomatic than Andrei.

"But that's not the case at all!" Kay cried. "Leah, you got just as much publicity." Leah wanted to kill Kay. Leah felt uncomfortable under the spotlight—unless she was performing—and she didn't want to make other people more jealous of her than they already were. Leah knew she was one of the Academy director's favorites, and everyone else knew it, too. Recently Leah had discovered that even the people who were now her best friends had hated her when she first turned up at the school. Leah couldn't help being a good dancer, but it hurt when it made other people—like teachers and partners—give her special treatment and made the other kids resent her.

But Kay wouldn't be put off, and she insisted that Leah turn the page again. "You are the only girl at SFBA who got a solo shot, Leah!" Katrina said, pointing to a photo heading up the third column. She sounded happy for Leah and not the least bit jealous.

Leah forced herself to look at the picture and felt a thrill of pride the minute she did. She couldn't wait to send a copy of the magazine to her mother. The photo captured Leah in a lovely, perfect arabesque. Leah bit her lip and gave an embarrassed little laugh. "It is a nice picture," she said.

"Good line!" Christopher Robson's voice startled her. In the excitement of the moment Leah had forgotten all about him. She glanced up nervously and shrunk back a little. She didn't trust Christopher. One minute he'd compliment her, the next he'd say something nasty. It never failed. That's why Pam dubbed him Dr. Jekyll and Mr. Hyde. But the look of approval on Christopher's face surprised Leah. He had already changed into his street clothes. He shifted his dance bag up on his shoulder and straightened the elegant cashmere scarf that peeked out from just inside his full-length leather coat. As he turned and headed for the door, he said, "But watch out, Stephenson. Pride cometh before a fall." He laughed and vanished through the door.

"Pleasant chap, isn't he?" Finola quipped, breaking an awkward bit of silence.

Andrei frowned. "He does not like you?" he asked Leah.

"He doesn't like anybody!" Linda Howe commented with a shrug. The leggy black girl smiled as she spotted her own picture, taken during rehearsals for an original ballet also choreographed for the gala.

"You look great in this picture, Katrina!" Kay commented. It was true: the delicate brown-haired dancer was caught at the peak of a delightful small jump as she led a group of girls across the floor in one of Madame's classes. "You look as if you're hanging from the air on wires."

"Like Taglioni," Alexandra pointed out. "You really should have been born last century. You look like those old lithographs in dance history books."

"And look at Pam!" Leah gasped, truly impressed. The small photo tucked at the bottom of the article's last page was breathtaking. The angle of the shot played up Pam's already incredible elevation. She was dancing with Alexandra, Mia, and several boys. The caption said something about how some girls outjump even the strongest boys, and Pam certainly was soaring high above the crowd. Leah turned around to congratulate Pam, but the redhead was nowhere in sight. Leah had seen Pam move away from the swarm of people, but she didn't think Pam had left the studio.

"Where is she?" she wondered aloud. Keeping her finger in the magazine to mark Pam's picture, Leah started toward the dressing room.

"Leah!" Kay cried after her. "Read this; they call you one of the most promising young dancers they've ever seen."

But Leah barely heard Kay. She was standing in the open dressing room door. Pam's Gucci dance bag and tall leather boots were missing from their regular spot. "Where *is* she?" Leah asked out loud, and wondered exactly where Pam had gone.

Chapter 3

"Leah Stephenson, you're dead wrong! You can't trust Pamela Hunter!" Kay Larkin exclaimed later that evening. Leah, Kay, and a group of other girls were gathered in Katrina Gray's spacious upstairs bedroom at the host family home where she and Finola Darling lived.

"I'm not talking about *trusting* Pam," Leah said. "I'm not about to hand her my secret diary or anything like that!" she snapped. She grabbed a handful of popcorn from the bowl in the center of the floor, popped one kernel into her mouth, then tossed the rest back peevishly and pulled the collar of her purple terry-cloth robe higher up around her neck. The room was well heated, but Leah felt cold and a little depressed. She stared down at the plush wall-to-wall pink carpet and absently ran her hand over it. When she looked up again, she stared directly at Kay, determined to try to make her friend understand. "I'm talking about being a little more considerate of her, that's all."

"Oh, spare me!" Linda moaned, and spread her

legs out in a perfect 180-degree angle, trying to stretch her turnout. She flopped forward, rested her cheek against the floor and regarded Leah coolly with doelike dark-brown eyes. "You've lost your marbles. Robson's getting to you, I can tell. No person in their right mind would even bother talking about a Be Kind to Pamela Hunter Week, much less do it."

"Come on, I'm not trying to 'be kind to Pam,' as if she's a kitten up for adoption," Leah said petulantly. "I'm only upset because we decided to have the party here." Leah glared at Linda, then looked away, knowing it was useless to try to convince her friends that Pam was worth worrying about.

"Thanks a lot!" Katrina said, pretending to look hurt.

"You know I didn't mean it like that." Leah reached over and patted Katrina's head. Linda and Kay had spent half the evening patiently plaiting Katrina's thick, frizzy hair into neat rows of corn curls, and it looked great. "I love coming over here to visit. It's fun, and Mrs. Wyndham is great. But let's be honest about it. Everyone knows the only reason we're here is so that we didn't have to invite Pam and Abby to our little slumber party."

"I do not see what is so strange about that," Alex said, shaking her head at Leah. The tall Russian girl stood up and stretched her arms high over her head. She hitched up her long black bathrobe and strolled over to the mirror. She opened her robe and turned to view her profile. First her right side, then her left. She smoothed the skinny white nightshirt down over her slim hips and sucked in her already flat tummy. Then she pressed her nose closer to the glass. Her strong features twisted up in a grimace of disgust, and she stuck her tongue out at her reflection. The effect of Finola's silver-white lipstick on her lips obviously didn't please her. "I look like a person from a tomb." She frowned and looked helplessly at Leah.

With a tired sigh Leah supplied the right word. "A ghost!"

"How do you bear wearing this stuff?" Alex asked Finola, and began to scrub off the gloss with a tissue. As she wiped her lips she addressed Leah's image in the mirror. "Leah, we all decided the issue of *FootNotes* was worth a major celebration. And last I heard, no one"—she paused and arched her finely tweezed eyebrows at Leah—"*no one* likes to have Pam or her sidekick Abigail at parties, any parties, if they can help it. I seem to remember you wanted to leave both Pam and Abby out of the surprise birthday party for Katrina last month."

"Touché!" Leah scrambled to her feet. Alex was right. Until recently, until last week actually, given a scale of one to ten of how cruel and obnoxious a person could be, Pam would have rated a thirty-one, with Christopher Robson close on her heels at twenty-eight. Leah folded her arms across her chest and strolled over to the window that overlooked the lush garden on the side of the house. She propped one knee on the window seat and stared out. How was she supposed to convince everyone of her new feelings for Pam when she didn't even understand them herself? Still, Leah felt that somehow, someway, she had to persuade her friends to give Pam a second, or a third, or a fourth chance.

Leah turned around and walked straight over to Alex. "I know," she said, leaning against the mirror while Alex continued to play with her makeup. "I used to feel that way about Pam. It's no secret. But I think—" She paused and pushed her longish bangs out of her eyes. "I think we've been wrong. The more I work with her on that pas de trois, the more I like her. I'm beginning to feel one of the reasons Pam's so hard-edged is to—I don't know." Leah groped for just the right word. "To protect herself. Yes, that's it." Leah ignored the groans coming from Kay's direction and went on. "She's a proud person. And leaving Pam out of things just makes her worse."

Kay pounced on Leah instantly. "So you admit it—she's bad to begin with."

"Why won't you listen?" Leah moaned and leaned back against the wall. She slid her back down the wall and sat on the floor. Propping her chin in her hands, she flashed Kay a look of despair. "You're hopeless, Larkin." She looked around the room at everyone. "I'm not blind to Pam. She's overly ambitious, and if you gave her the chance for a juicy part in a performance, she'd probably kill for it. But I don't think she's *all* bad. Besides, Andrei said—"

"Andrei?" Alex asked, looking away from her reflection for the first time in ten minutes. "I cannot imagine Andrei has very much to say about that girl."

"No, Andrei doesn't usually talk about Pam, you're right. But one night when he was helping me rehearse for the Louise Adams competition, he said something about Pam. For some reason it stuck with me," Leah explained.

Katrina poured herself a glass of juice. "I didn't think he knew her well enough to talk about."

"He doesn't. Just from repertory class," Leah admitted. "But he said he felt sorry for her."

Katrina practically choked on her juice. "Sorry for her?" she blurted out. After a moment's stunned silence all the girls except Leah burst out laughing.

"Poor, poor Pamela!" Kay mugged a sad face and mimed playing a violin. "She's only the richest kid in the school."

"That is not the point!" Alex broke in. "She's the meanest person at SFBA."

Katrina frowned at Alex's blunt description of Pam. "That's not fair, Alex. I don't know if she's mean so much as competitive. Like Leah said, she'd probably kill someone to get a part. It's just in competitive situations that she's at her worst."

"Tell me about it!" Suzanne spoke up from the rocking chair, where she sat sewing ribbons on a stack of new toe shoes. "In class this morning she stepped on my foot—on purpose, I swear it—just to get to the front of the line during those brisés from the corner."

Before Leah could respond to Suzanne's accusation, Alex spoke up again. "No, Katrina is right. I was unfair. But Pam is not *just* competitive. I am competitive. I will do anything to get a part, too. I will work hard. I will dance my heart out." Alex paused, then admitted with obvious reluctance, "I will be extra nice to the teacher."

"But you aren't like Pam at all," Kay declared loyally.

Suzanne poked up her glasses and put aside her sewing. "Lucky for us, Pam's one of a kind."

"I can't say I'd like a whole school full of Pams," Leah agreed, and flopped down in the middle of Katrina's four-poster. She stared up at the ruffled canopy. "Pam's more extreme about having to be on top," she mused, "but I'm sure there's a reason." Before anyone could object to that, Leah hurried on. "She's got problems—that's what Andrei suspects. Andrei thinks she hates to dance."

"Andrei needs a doctor for the head!" Alex scoffed.

"A psychologist," Kay filled in for her.

"Whatever," Alex said impatiently. "Andrei is one of my very oldest friends. He is also stupid when it comes to people," Alex said as she let down her long black hair and reached for her brush. "I think when it comes to Pam, Andrei has a blind spot." She craned her neck and peeked through the open door into the hall. Mrs. Wyndham was nowhere in sight. When she went on, she lowered her voice. "You know the woman Andrei will marry."

"Claire DuParc?" Suzanne asked.

Alex nodded. "She has red hair like Pamela. Maybe Andrei has a thing for girls with red hair."

Leah groaned. Lately Alex had developed a one-track mind. In the past few weeks she had taken to posing in front of mirrors, constantly reapplying her makeup, and talking about guys whenever they had free time. Not that Alex had enough free time to date—like most of the girls at SFBA she was too busy, and the nights she wasn't rehearsing or being coached she was usually just too tired to go out. Alex knew as well as Leah that Andrei was not interested in Pam or in any other "little girls" in the school, as he called them. Still, Alex had had a childhood crush on the dancer, and Leah suspected she still had her dreams about Andrei—despite his engagement.

Leah slipped off the bed and headed toward the french doors that led out to the terrace. The

Wyndhams' house stood high on a hill, and Katrina's small balcony looked out onto the city below. Leah gazed at the beautiful view, trying to think of a way to cut through everyone's prejudice against Pam.

Katrina seemed to sense her mood. "Leah," she said softly, "it's really sweet of you to want to get to know Pam better, to include her in things and all. But you of all people should know what she's like. Look what happened to you during audition week!"

Leah nodded her head, then turned around slowly. "Believe me, I won't forget what she did." She looked down at her feet and wriggled her big toe. Her bunion was aching, and little red bruises dotted the ends of the other toes, the results of too much rehearsing and not enough rest. Leah let her mind drift back to the first time she had met Pam, in September. Pam's energy, strong personality, and technique had impressed Leah. For the first few days, before the entrance audition, Pam had pretended to be Leah's friend. But come audition day, Pam had shocked everyone by stealing Leah's carefully prepared piece and performing it in front of the judges only moments before Leah herself was scheduled to go on. Leah had felt betrayed, hurt, and very angry. She was most angry at herself for not having seen through Pam, and she had promised herself she would never speak to Pam again. Leah knew from firsthand experience how backstabbing and tricky Pam could be. Still, that didn't change her feelings now.

"I don't know about the rest of you," Leah finally said, "but I'm convinced if we were just a little nicer to Pam that she'd start being a little nicer to us. I think she's a pretty decent person under that shell."

"I think you're wrong," Finola said. "I don't know Pam as well as the rest of you do, but she gives me the creeps sometimes. The less I have to do with Pamela Hunter, the better."

Alex gave a proud toss of her head and eyed Leah carefully. She wagged a finger under Leah's nose and warned, "I do not know about Pam and rehearsals—"

"She sure can stand up to Mr. Robson!" Linda interrupted.

"She's the only one who's tough enough to deal with him," Suzanne said. "But that doesn't make me like her any better."

"Whatever," Alex said impatiently, "I think you better be careful, Leah. However Pam has been acting lately, that article in *FootNotes* is going to make her show her true flag."

"Huh?" several girls said at once.

"You know. You see what she really feels inside, not what she pretends," Alex said, annoyed that no one understood her.

"Her true *colors*," Kay corrected, then turned to Leah. "And Pam's true color is green—with jealousy. Just wait. Your solo shot in *FootNotes* is going to stir up a hornet's nest as far as Pamela Hunter's concerned."

Leah lay flat on her back in her sleeping bag on Finola's bedroom floor, staring at the ceiling. The tightly drawn curtains blotted out the city lights, and Leah's eyes peered up into almost complete darkness. From across the long narrow room Leah could hear Finola's steady, peaceful breathing.

Leah's whole body was crying for sleep. Every muscle in her back and legs ached. But her mind was racing as she considered Kay's warning about

Pam. Some voice inside of Leah said that Kay was right. Pamela Hunter might have turned over a new leaf—being supportive of Leah and everyone else during Robson's rehearsals was certainly evidence of that. But Leah knew Pam had to be very jealous of Leah's featured position in the *FootNotes* article. Because in Pam's shoes, Leah would be, too.

Leah rolled over on her side and closed her eyes. For a minute she seemed to see Pam's face, then it shifted to the face of another girl with red hair, and Leah's eyes eyes popped open again. What in the world made her start thinking about Chrissy Morely, her best friend from back home? Chrissy might be a redhead, but she wasn't at all like Pam. Leah's childhood friend was a little on the chubby side, and she had a face full of freckles and sparkling brown eyes. She was a whiz at science and math and had suffered through ballet for seven years with Leah at Hannah Greene's School of Dance and Theater Arts. Chrissy was a student at San Lorenzo High now, and in spite of her thick weekly letters, Leah missed her a lot. She certainly wasn't as pretty as Pam, but she was a much nicer person. But Leah hadn't always known that. In fact, Leah hadn't thought about how she'd become friends with Chrissy for years now.

Leah's parents had moved from Los Angeles to San Lorenzo when Leah was in the second grade, and Chrissy had been her new next-door neighbor. Leah hated Chrissy at first sight: she was brainy, wore glasses, and tended to stuff awful things like frogs and worms into her pockets. It was pretty obvious that Chrissy didn't like Leah, either. Miss Melissa Curtis, the meanest teacher in Hilltop Elementary, had been the second grade teacher. She seemed to sense that Chrissy and Leah hated each other, and she was so mean that she made them sit together on purpose. That made them both hate Miss Curtis even more. But hating Miss Curtis did a funny thing to Leah and Chrissy: it gave them something to talk about on the way home. And before Leah knew it, she had forgotten all about Chrissy's worms and found that Chrissy had become her best friend. The little girl she had hated because she wore glasses and was in the "gifted" section of the class for math, while Leah was put in the slow-learners group, turned out to be the best friend Leah had ever had. Now that she thought about it, it was funny that she got to know Chrissy because of a mean teacher. And now she was getting to know Pam better only because of Mr. Robson, another mean teacher.

Of course, Leah wasn't seven years old anymore, and she didn't exactly expect sessions with Christopher Robson to lead to the blossoming of a friendship between her and Pam. But she was beginning to admire the southern girl more, and Leah's experience with Chrissy had proved one thing at least. People definitely weren't what they seemed on the surface. Pam appeared to be a self-centered girl, ready to antagonize anyone who got in her way. But Andrei's comment about Pam made Leah wonder if there wasn't more to her than that. She was almost certain Pam wasn't as bad as everyone thought—including herself.

Leah's eyes grew heavy, and the arguments inside her head began to blur and finally fade away. She decided that if Pam was jealous, Leah would know about it first thing tomorrow in class.

Leah would have a chance to check out what Kay called Pam's true colors then.

Leah drifted into a restless dream, one that starred Pamela Hunter. The redhead was on a small stage right in the middle of SFBA's Red Studio. She was wearing a jet-black tutu, like the Black Swan's in the third act of *Swan Lake*, but she was dancing the wrong steps. It wasn't Odile's flashy variation at all; instead, it was something dainty and very familiar to Leah. Leah was sitting in the rear of the audience, and she wanted to yell out to Pam and tell her she was dancing the wrong solo. But she couldn't find her voice, and with a crazy smile on her face Pam continued to stab her way through the delicate choreography. She had the phrasing all wrong, but Leah knew how it should be danced. Then she realized that Pam was dancing Leah's variation from the pas de trois they had been rehearsing for weeks now— she had stolen Leah's role and was making a mess of it. But that didn't bother Leah half as much as Pamela's hair did. Beneath a sparkly tiara, thick waves hung loose down Pam's back, reaching all the way to her waist. But her hair wasn't red anymore. Pam had dyed it bright green.

Chapter 4

"Is that a frog I see before me?" Finola Darling quipped the next morning as Pam paraded into Madame Preston's class in the Red Studio.

"Could have fooled me," Kay shot back. "I do believe that sight over yonder is just Pamela Hunter in a kelly-green leotard."

"A green leotard!" Alex repeated, amazed. She chuckled and turned to Leah, who was sprawled facedown on the floor, kicking her legs up one at a time behind her, doing her own particular series of preclass warm-ups. "Leah, you must not miss the explosion that will happen now. Madame never, ever, in the three years I have been here, let a girl take her class in anything other than pink tights and black leotard. Never."

Leah propped herself up on her elbows and craned her neck to sneak a peek at the front of the room. Through sleepy eyes she watched Madame discuss the day's music with Robert. "What's this about Pam?" she said with a yawn. Then she saw Pam. Leah's eyes popped open and she was

33

instantly wide awake. She straightened up and sat back on her knees. "I don't believe it!"

The horror in her voice made Alex frown. "Leah, what's wrong?"

"The leotard Pam's wearing is green." Leah's eyes were riveted on the redhead as she paraded right up to Madame and stood with her hands folded primly in front of her.

Linda laughed and tickled Leah in the ribs. "Stephenson, wake up. What do you think Kay and Finola were talking about just now?"

Leah gave Linda a helpless look. How could she explain about the green leotard being the exact same color as Pam's hair in her dream last night? It seemed to Leah like some sort of omen. So Kay was right after all. That *FootNotes* article was all Pam needed to show her true colors, and she was going to cause trouble. The fact that Pam was wearing green today, against all school regulations, proved it.

Neither Leah nor her friends were in earshot of Pam when Madame finally looked up and spotted Pam's outfit. The gray-haired woman straightened her back and frowned. Pam clasped her hands together in a meek, pleading gesture. Leah couldn't imagine what Pam's excuse was: she had more leotards than any of the other girls. Surely she couldn't say she didn't have a clean one.

As Pam went through what looked to be a very lengthy explanation, Madame's stony expression began to soften. Whatever Pam was giving as an excuse was working. Kay whistled under her breath. "How does that girl do it? She calls Leah a teacher's pet, when she's the one who gets away with murder."

"A green leotard is not murder!" Alex sniffed. "But Pam tends to get away with a lot more than just wearing the wrong thing to class. Madame is being very unfair to everyone else she ever punished for breaking dress codes. Tomorrow we should *all* come to class in green."

Any other day Leah would have laughed at Alex's rebellious plan. Her Russian friend's passion for honesty sometimes got carried a bit too far. Today, however, Leah barely paid attention to Alex. She kept watching Pam, wondering what the redhead would do next.

Leah didn't have to wonder long. Pam's interview with Madame was over quickly, and, swinging her overstuffed Gucci dance bag from the fingers of one hand, she strutted toward the back of the room, grinning in Leah's direction.

Stopping just short of Leah, Pam set her dance bag down and with a firm shove sent it sliding across the floor, where it landed in a pile of assorted sweatshirts and bags heaped in front of a small supply closet. She dropped down next to Leah and stretched her shapely legs straight out in front of her. She leaned forward from her hip joints and stretched her torso over her legs.

"Leah Stephenson, I do declare, that photo of you and Andrei in *FootNotes* is marvelous!" She leaned her forehead on her knee and grabbed her ankles with her hands to stretch the backs of her thighs even further. "That should show Robson, shouldn't it? And in that arabesque on the last page, you look like a blond Margot Fonteyn."

Leah stopped her own warm-ups and gaped at Pam. Pam met Leah's eyes without blinking, and her smile seemed warm and genuine. Pam sounded sincere and not the least bit sarcastic. "You really mean that?" Leah asked.

Kay let out a little groan and got up. "Time to get to the barre, girls. Madame's going to start any minute. It's getting stuffy down here on the floor, anyway."

Pam looked up. "Kay, did you say something? I didn't quite catch it."

"Nothing worth catching, Pam. Nothing at all," Kay shot back over her shoulder, and hurried off. Finola got up next, then Alex. They waited a second for Leah to join them, and when she didn't, Alex narrowed her dark almond-shaped eyes and shook her head.

Leah saw her and understood exactly what Alex wanted her to do—to get up and leave Pam sitting there by herself. Leah didn't move. For once Leah was not going to treat Pam as if she had the plague. She had just complimented Leah, and to Leah's ear Pam sounded as if she meant it. The least Leah could do was give Pam a chance. In a voice loud enough for Alex and Finola to hear, Leah said, "Talking about great photos, Pam, the one of you makes you look like you can outjump even Andrei."

Pam eyed Leah suspiciously. "You mean that?"

Leah pointedly ignored the skeptical note in Pam's voice. "Of course I do." Pam smiled, and for a minute she looked like a little girl, innocent and happy. Leah could see the side of Pam that Pam had been hiding, and Leah liked it, a lot.

"Thanks, Leah," Pam said shyly.

Madame clapped her hands, and Leah sprang to her feet. "To the barre, girls," Madame ordered.

An hour and a half later Leah hurried to the

back of the Red Studio to get a new pair of pointe shoes out of her bag. The regular part of morning class was over, and it was time for Madame's special twice-a-week pointe class for the girls. Leah flopped down on the floor and took advantage of the five-minute break between sessions to fix her hair. Kay sat down beside her and stared at the dirty toe shoe she held in her hand.

"I don't know how you do it, but somehow your shoes never get quite as messed up as mine."

"That's not true," Leah protested with a laugh. "I go through a pair of shoes every two days just because of Robson's rehearsals." She rummaged in her purple dance bag again and produced another shoe. The box of the toe was hopelessly broken, and a blue Magic Marker had leaked all over the once pale pink satin.

Kay gawked at the shoe. "That doesn't look like you rehearsed in it. It looks like you took an exam in it!"

Leah laughed again. She was feeling very light and happy after class. This morning's session had gone well so far on a couple of fronts. Madame had singled her out for praise twice, complimenting the perfect rhythm of her frappés at the barre, and remarking that her balance during adagio work was worthy of Fonteyn. When Madame said that, Leah couldn't help but glance in Pam's direction. The redhead gave her the thumbs-up sign, and Leah finished her adagio work feeling satisfied. Pam's behavior this morning was proof enough to Leah's mind that Kay was wrong about the southern girl. Now all Leah had to do was get Kay to admit that.

"Kay," Leah started, "about Pam—" Leah paused

to pick up her right shoe. From superstition or maybe just habit, Leah always put on her right shoe first. She wrapped a small padding of lambswool around the ends of her toes and wriggled her foot into the satin slipper. "I think you're—*eek!*"

Leah's shriek echoed throughout the studio. Leah kicked her foot, and her new toe shoe went sailing through the air, landing in the middle of the room with a thud. Something gray and fuzzy rolled out.

"Ooh!" Linda yelped, jumping out of the way of the round gray object. "What is it?"

"A mouse!" Katrina pronounced. She walked up to Leah's shoe and prodded the ball of gray fur with her finger. "It's dead," she informed everyone with a relieved smile.

"A mouse!" several girls screeched at once.

"Stephenson, what is the meaning of this?" Madame's stern voice broke through the chorus of scared voices and cries of disgust.

Leah got to her feet. She gaped in horror at her other new shoe, which poked out of her bag. She couldn't help wondering exactly what lurked in the depths of its blocked toe. Finally she braved a glance at Madame. "I—I don't know," she said, and began to shiver. "I was talking to Kay, and I put my shoe on, and my foot—my foot—" Leah's voice broke, and her stomach began to churn. She felt as if she was going to be sick. "My foot wouldn't go in. Something was squishy and soft and then I knew it wasn't lambswool—"

"That's enough, Leah," Madame broke in. Leah looked up quickly. The corners of Madame's straight, thin lips were turning up in the barest hint of a smile. Leah couldn't believe it: Madame actually thought finding a mouse in your shoes was funny!

"Robert—" the gray-haired teacher began, then actually looked surprised when she saw Katrina pick up the mouse by its tail. "Katrina, you don't mind getting rid of this"—she paused to find just the right word, and said with some distaste—"this corpse!"

A nervous titter went through the room, and this time Madame didn't even bother to hold back her smile. It was obvious the mouse disgusted her, but she also seemed to find some humor in the situation—unlike Leah.

Katrina carried the mouse at arm's length out into the hall and was quickly back again.

"How could you, Katrina?" Alex asked, wrinkling her nose.

Katrina laughed. "I'm from farm country in Vermont. Mice are pretty common around there," she said, and walked over to her bag. She pulled out a wad of tissue and wiped her hands.

"Leah's from a farm, too!" Linda reminded her.

Leah turned red. "Yes, I am. And I'm not afraid of mice most of the time," she insisted. "But sticking your toe in a shoe and finding one is not very pleasant." Leah straightened up a little, her pride injured. "I just don't know how it got there."

"Maybe your cat, Misha, put it there!" Pam suggested helpfully. She was warming up her feet at the barre and seemed oddly calm about the presence of the mouse. "Cats often bring mice as presents to their owners."

"Spare me!" Alex moaned. "And what do you know about cats anyway? Until Leah brought Misha to the boardinghouse, you never lived with a cat—at least that's what you told us then."

Before Pam could explain, Madame broke in. "Okay, girls. I don't think anyone knows how the mouse got there. That is not the point. The point is we are here to dance, no, Leah? Hurry, hurry." She tapped her finger against her wristwatch. "I do not have all day."

"Yes, Madame," Leah said obediently, and picked up the other shoe. She worked up the nerve to peek inside, then she rapped it against the floor, conscious that all the other girls were watching her.

"Let me," Katrina said, and took the shoe from Leah. She bravely poked her hand in and pulled it out again. "It's safe."

Leah laughed at Katrina's expression and put the shoe on her left foot. Then she sat perplexed on the floor. "But Madame," she said, looking toward the front of the room. "I don't have another shoe—one that's not broken."

Madame frowned. "You have that one." She pointed to the shoe lying in the middle of the floor.

"You want me to put that back on?" Leah asked, incredulous.

The faint smile on the stern teacher's face faded. "Why not?"

"Because—" Leah started to answer, then caught Alex's eye. Alex seemed to be warning Leah with a subtle shake of her head.

"Yes, Madame. I will put it on." Leah forced herself to walk across the floor. Knowing that every girl in the room felt for her didn't make it any easier. Leah couldn't explain why, but putting on a shoe that had recently been home to a dead mouse certainly seemed like the worst thing that could happen in ballet class.

Suddenly Pam walked away from the barre and picked up the shoe before Leah got to it. "Here," she said, handing it to Leah. Her green eyes were all sympathy. "Just—just try to put it out of you mind. It's gone now."

"Uh—yes. You're right," Leah murmured. The rest of the class went back to the barre and began exercises to warm up their feet. Standing on one leg, Leah closed her eyes and forced herself to put on the shoe. Her toes wriggled as she slipped her foot beneath the band of pink elastic she had sewn around the ankle. Leah put her foot down on the floor and bent over to tie her ribbon. When she finished, she experimented with a pirouette on her right toe.

The shoe was fine, but the mouse had done a good job of ruining her class. Before she changed her shoes and encountered the mouse, Leah had been having a great day. Now everything began going wrong.

"Leah, what do you think you are doing?" Madame finally stopped the music and pointed at Leah. "You go right back to the barre and practice your echappés. I have never seen you overcross your fifth like that before. You will get hurt like that. It is a bad habit."

"Sorry," Leah murmured. She blushed and hurried over to the barre. She faced the wooden rail and stood very still, waiting for the music to begin again. Though her back was to the room, she could see Madame's face in the mirror.

"Real dancers," Madame continued in a tight,

annoyed voice, "do not let anything get in the way of their dancing. During the war in London, when there was bombing every night, the dancers kept performing. They let nothing interfere with their art. To think a girl like you would let a little thing like a mouse rattle you so." Madame shook her head and tugged down the jacket of her pale tweed suit. "You disappoint me, Leah. I had expected more from you."

Chapter 5

"I never knew Misha caught mouses!" Alex commented after class. She, Leah, and Kay were hurrying down the back stairs of the school to get their mail from the campus post office.

"Mice!" Kay corrected. "Misha should catch mice. He's still a kitten, but he's big and strong. I think he's going to be a very big cat!"

"Like in the zoo!" Alex laughed at her own joke, but Leah was not amused. Madame's class had been a disaster, a perfect disaster. Leah had totally fallen apart during pointe work. She hadn't done one thing right and she had spent more than half the class at the barre, wasting precious time doing careful echappés while the rest of the girls got to practice their fouéttés. Leah had the sinking feeling that performing badly in one class would make her fall terribly behind. And SFBA was too competitive a school for that.

"So when he catches a mice, does he bring it to you?" Alex asked.

"If he caught mice, he would bring them to me, yes. I'm sure he would," Leah snapped. She stopped halfway down the stairs and hoisted her dance bag up her shoulder. "Why are you suddenly so interested in Misha, Miss Sorokin?"

Leah's seething anger didn't faze Alex at all. She stood a couple of steps below Leah and favored her with a smile. "I can understand a cat bringing a present to you. A pet thinks you are its mother. But I cannot understand a cat opening a dance bag, finding a brand new toe shoe, and putting the mouse in that very shoe. The one you had to wear for Madame's Saturday pointe class. That would have to be a very smart cat."

Kay suddenly seemed to get Alex's drift. "You mean a very catty cat, don't you, Alex? One with red hair and a green leotard?"

Leah pushed her way past Alex. "Why would Pamela Hunter put a mouse in my shoe?" Leah called over her shoulder. On the bottom step she turned around and waited for Alex.

Alex's dark eyes looked very serious. "Because she wants you to be upset. Because she wants Madame to be upset with you, like she was in class today. That has never happened before, not to you. Madame embarrassed you, no?"

"Oh, I've had my differences with Madame before. Besides, I was to blame, not Pam. Anyway," Leah said, suddenly remembering, "I never leave my toe shoes in my bag overnight. I leave them out on the window. Misha could have easily jumped up on the sill and hidden a mouse in one of them."

Neither Kay nor Alex looked convinced. "Look," Leah continued, "can either of you picture Pamela Hunter killing a mouse—or even picking up a dead one that just happened to be lying around the boardinghouse—and actually handling it with her perfectly manicured fingers?"

Alex laughed. "That is a good point. The mystery deepens."

Before Leah could reply to that, Kay said, "I think if Pam wanted something badly enough, she would do anything to get it. And she's angry about *FootNotes*. I just know it. I told you something like this would happen."

Leah dropped her bag on the floor and threw both hands up in the air. "You heard Pam today. She wasn't upset about the article at all. Why should she be? I got a solo shot, sure, but her picture makes her look like the best dancer in the school." Leah knew her last comment was a little mean, since Alex was hardly visible in most of the pictures. Normally Leah would never rub something like that in, especially when it came to Alex, who was Leah's best friend. But Kay's and Alex's attitude toward Pam really bothered Leah, and she wasn't in the mood to be nice.

If Leah's comment hurt Alex, the Russian girl didn't show it. She simply shook her head at Leah. "Be careful of Pam. She is not the way she seemed today. She is not happy about *FootNotes*. Why should she be? I'm not happy either, and I am your friend."

Kay looked from Leah to Alex and cleared her throat. "We're all friends, and like you always said, Alex, we can stay friends in spite of the competition around here if we work at it. Right?"

"I don't think Alex is worried about the three of us staying friends," Leah commented.

"No, I am not. But speaking of friends," Alex said as they hurried down the hall toward the post office, "should you not get a letter from Chrissy soon? It seems like a long time since her last one."

Leah nodded sadly. "Tell me about it! I don't think I've gotten any mail for about a week and a half now, maybe longer."

The SFBA post office was actually a converted supply closet with a double door. The top of the door was open, and a pretty, brown-haired young dancer was sitting on a chair, sorting mail into cubbyholes.

"Hi, Emily." Kay greeted the company member warmly and propped her elbow on the edge of the door. "Any mail from home, from Mars, from anywhere would be nice."

Emily Dowson returned Kay's grin and reached up to a top cubbyhole. "You're in luck once again—in fact I'm beginning to wonder if you're out for the most-letters-received-in-a-year award." Emily rifled through the handful of envelopes before handing them to Kay. "You've got a couple from your mom, I think." Kay's natural mother was the internationally famous ballerina, Lynne Vreeland. Until a couple of months ago no one at SFBA had known of Kay's relationship to the star, but now that everyone did, people were always asking Kay about Miss Vreeland.

"I'll tell you all the hot news as soon as I read them, Emily," Kay assured Emily.

"Here's your mail, Alex," Emily said, handing her a couple of airmail letters. She made a sad face when she saw Leah anxiously waiting. "Sorry, Leah. I don't get it. Your mail was always so regular."

Leah was disappointed, but she tried to explain the lack of letters to her friends. "Chrissy's probably busy with midterms, and who knows what's going on with my mom. I bet she's got some hot new business deal and is working all hours of the day and night. I'm sure something will turn up soon," she concluded with more confidence than she felt.

"Is that clock right?" Kay suddenly squealed.

"Better not be," Alex groaned.

"Corps rehearsal started ten minutes ago!" Leah cried. "And I've got a costume fitting first."

"See ya later!" Kay yelled, and bolted back up the stairs with Alex following fast on her heels.

Leah tore down the low-ceilinged hall and skidded to a stop in front of the door that led to the wardrobe and sewing rooms. The door was open and loud voices carried out into the hall. Leah stopped when she heard Pam, and for a moment found herself wondering if Alex was right and she was wrong. Pam's voice sounded so angry. It was the voice of someone capable of some pretty dirty tricks. But Leah wasn't going to lose her newfound faith in Pam, not yet.

"Sorry I'm late," Leah cried. She tossed her dance bag down and hurried behind the antique Chinese screen Madame had donated to the wardrobe mistress to curtain off a changing area for the girls.

Mrs. Slavinska's motherly voice called over the screen, "You take your time, Leah. You are easy to fit."

"And what's that supposed to mean?" Pam asked icily. Leah poked her head around the screen in time to see Pam squirming into the bodice of her tutu for the first act. The heavily embroidered and beaded rust-colored bodice was too tight, and Madame would never let one of her students dance in something that low cut—not at a scholarship performance with an audience full of benefactors.

"It means, Pamela," Mrs. Slavinska said curtly, "that Leah never changes her size from one fitting to the next. You are getting too big for this. I must alter it again. But the performance is Thursday, and I will not alter it one more time." She patted Pam on the rear end and sent her back behind the screen, where Leah was quickly folding up her purple overalls.

"I am not getting fat," Pam insisted. "That woman just does not know how to sew for a girl who has a real figure. That's all. I'm trim as can be."

"Of course you are, Pam," Leah soothed. "Maybe she got the costumes mixed up."

The words were barely out of Leah's mouth, when Mrs. Stravinska said, "Oh! Pamela, I am sorry. I give you the wrong costume. Leah, put on that bodice."

"See," Pam gloated. From behind the screen she stuck out her tongue in the wardrobe mistress's direction.

A plump hand poked around the corner of the screen and held out another bodice that Pam took. It was a more coppery shade of satin than Leah's. Leah stepped into the one Pam had just taken off—it fit perfectly. She came out from behind the screen and smiled at Mrs. Slavinska. "It's wonderful," she said.

"I like better when you wear something pink. But the set is all this rusty forest color and there are no pink or blue or colors right for you. I think these costumes from old company productions are too heavy for young girls, but there is no money for new ones." Mrs. Slavinska poked her head into an open wicker truck and pulled out a tutu. The top layer was satin and beaded and the same shade of rust as Leah's bodice. The tulle underskirts were tinted paler shades of pinky rust. Leah loved the costume, and when she stepped into it, she stood a little taller. Putting on a tutu always made Leah feel more like a ballerina and less like a dance student. Mrs. Slavinska fastened the back for Leah and began to pin extra fabric over Leah's slim hips.

"Don't I get one of those?" Pam said, coming out from behind the screen. She craned her neck and looked into the trunk. She fingered the costumes hanging on the rack, and her hand lingered on a very full white tutu that Leah knew had to be Katrina's.

"Don't touch. If it gets dirty, I have to clean before poor little Katrina gets to wear it." She rapped the back of Pam's hands with her tape measure and glared at the girl. "As for you," Mrs. Slavinska said sharply, "I send you onstage just like that, all bodice and just pink tights." She looked up at Pam, who was still eyeing Katrina's costume greedily.

Pam flopped down on the bench and looked at Leah. "Doesn't it bother you just an eensy-teensy bit to know Katrina gets a new costume while we get these ratty old hand-me-downs?"

Mrs. Slavinska didn't give Leah a chance to answer. "The star of the performance gets the new costume. You are not the star. Not this time," she pointed out.

Pam dropped her eyes and began to sulk.

A burst of static came from somewhere just above the costume rack, and Leah jumped. She had forgotten the school even had a public address system. Madame hated it and used it only in emergencies. "Slavinska," Madame said. "Come up to the office at once. There is a problem down at the opera house. I think you may have to rush over there with Raul to fix everything up before curtain time."

Mrs. Slavinska muttered something in Russian. With a defeated shrug of her shoulders she pocketed her glasses and said, "I must go now. You come back tomorrow. I will have this finished then. I think your skirt will fit, Pamela. But I check again tomorrow. Do not bother with lights. I will come back later.'

The small energetic woman bustled down the hall, and Pam turned her back to Leah. "Unzip me."

"I wonder if we're too late for rehearsal upstairs," Leah said in a worried voice. She was trying carefully not to catch Pam's zipper on any of the loose threads that stuck out every which way from the newly altered seams.

"I'm thinking of skipping it," Pam said. She sank back down on the bench and propped her feet up on the wicker trunk.

"You think we can?" Leah asked, struggling to undo her own zipper.

Pam just shrugged, and the straps of her bodice fell down on her arms. "If I dance one more step today, I'm going to drop."

Leah felt the same way herself. She hesitated. She had never purposely skipped a rehearsal before. "When Madame announced rehearsal schedules, she did say that sometimes we'd miss some sessions because of costume fittings or or conflicting coaching sessions."

"Yes, she did. So she can't be upset with us, Leah." Pam got up and stretched. The back of her costume gaped open, but Pam didn't seem to care. "Want a soda or juice?" Pam fumbled in the outside pocket of her dance bag and pulled out some change.

"You're going out to the machine like that?" Leah said, shocked.

"No one's around. Besides, what difference does it make? It's just my bare back. I've worn bathing suits skimpier than this."

"Okay, I'll take a diet soda, then," Leah said, looking for her bag. Pam waved her off and paraded into the hallway. A few minutes later she was back. She opened her bottle of apple juice and tossed Leah her can of soda.

Leah downed some soda, then looked around the cramped wardrobe room. Three sewing machines were open, and tutus in various stages of completion occupied each one. Wicker trunks were stacked up to the ceiling, and bins of fabrics, trimmings, and feathers were stacked on shelves against the wall. Pam got up and sauntered over to the closet that opened off the main room. Leah followed, curious. She hadn't been down in wardrobe much, and the closet had never been open before. Racks of costumes lined the sides, and more trunks and interesting-looking boxes were stored underneath.

Leah strolled down the row of costumes and stopped in front of the mirror. Beside the full-length mirror was an old-fashioned redwood dresser, and above it an oval-framed old photograph caught Leah's eye. A young woman's face looked back at her with huge, sad eyes. The girl looked like she was about seventeen, and looking at her picture, Leah had the uncanny feeling she was staring back at Leah. Leah shifted her gaze to the frame itself. Its small bit of metal scrollwork bore the name Letitia Moorehouse.

"Have you heard about Letitia?"

"Oh, Pam," Leah gasped, her heart suddenly racing. "I forgot you were here." She turned around and grinned sheepishly. In the time Leah had been looking at the portrait, Pam had changed back into her skinny black stretch pants and a thick patterned sweater. She was pulling a brush through her hair, and Leah felt happy that Pam had dyed it green only in a dream.

"I didn't mean to scare you, Leah," Pam said smoothly. "All I said was, do you know who Letitia is?"

Leah cocked her head. "I don't think so."

"Here." Pam handed Leah her overalls and T-shirt and then sat on a narrow bench. "Get dressed and I'll tell you all about it. I thought everyone around the school had heard about Letitia."

"Not me. Go ahead." Leah stepped out of the tutu and pulled on her overalls.

"It's a romance, of course," Pam said.

Leah pulled her T-shirt on and adjusted the straps of her overalls. She sat down across from Pam, where she could still see the picture of Letitia.

"Back in the old days they called her Letty. Letty Moorehouse was the only daughter of a very rich railroad baron. Mr. Eliah Moorehouse was the richest man in all of San Francisco, and he built this mansion."

"Was this before the earthquake?" Leah asked.

Pam frowned. "Now, don't interrupt me. I'll get mixed up. It's an old story, and I want to tell it just like I heard it when I got here."

Leah wanted to ask Pam who had told her the story. It had probably been Diana Chang, one of the principals with the Bay Area Ballet and the one teacher at the school who favored the strong-willed redhead.

"But yes, it was before the earthquake. Or part of the story is," Pam corrected herself. "Letty was the most beautiful girl in town and the belle of every ball. But she had a secret passion for dance. When she was young her father sent her to France, and Letty saw ballet for the very first time."

"She was a dancer!" Leah gasped, her eyes shining. She had felt a subtle kinship with the girl in the picture, and now she knew why.

"No—not exactly. When she came home her father forbade her to dance ballet. In those days being a ballet dancer was considered very improper for a young lady."

"How sad."

"Oh, it gets much sadder. Letty pleaded and pleaded, until her father finally gave in and allowed her to have a ballet instructor. He was a handsome young man, and his name was Pierre. He had come to the Bay Area a few years before. He coached Letty privately. And of course—"

"They fell in love!"

"Yes, they did. I told you this was a real romance."

"Then what happened?"

"If you stop interrupting me, I'll tell you," Pam said, frowning at Leah. "Letty and Pierre hid their love from her father, knowing he would never allow them to marry. One day Pierre came to visit Letty, and they stole away to the greenhouse—the same greenhouse that stands along the west wall of the mansion now. Letty was in Pierre's arms when the ground began to shake."

"*The* earthquake?" Leah's hand flew to her mouth in horror. "Did they die?"

"No—not right away. Pierre was brave, and he rushed back into the house to save Letty's mother. But he and Mrs. Moorehouse were buried in the rubble when there was another tremor. Letty lived, but it would have been better if she had died."

"Why?" Leah asked.

"Broken-hearted, Letty wandered around the grounds, calling out for her mother and Pierre. She finally went mad and threw herself off the cliff into the waters of the Bay." Pam clasped her hands in front of her and looked up at the ceiling. She let out a loud, sad sigh.

Leah dropped her gaze. "That's the worst story I ever heard."

Pam's eyes narrowed. "What do you mean?"

"It's so sad."

"Oh. I thought for a minute you didn't believe me."

"Not believe you?" Leah looked up, dazed. "Why wouldn't I believe you?"

"Because—because that's not the end of the story," Pam said hurriedly. She gave convincing little shudder and wrapped her arms around her chest. "Letty didn't die—not completely."

Leah stared at the picture and frowned. "You mean—" she said, the meaning of Pam's words finally dawning on her. She turned back to Pam. "You mean that she's a ghost?" Pam looked so absolutely serious that Leah had to stifle the impulse to laugh. She prided herself in not being superstitious. Most of the dancers she knew believed in all sorts of jinxes and good luck charms, and Alex was even hooked on seeing her future in tea leaves.

Pam shrugged. "Now, you know me. I'm a very practical sort of girl. I don't even own a rabbit's foot or anything dumb like that. I certainly never believed in ghosts—until now. But I've seen her!" Pam declared solemnly. "With my very own eyes."

"Pamela Hunter—you've actually seen the ghost of Letty Moorehouse?" Leah asked. Ghosts didn't quite seem the sort of thing a girl like Pamela Hunter would put much faith in. Any ghost Pam saw would have to be real.

At first Pam replied to Leah's question with only a vigorous nod. Then she looked around and beckoned Leah closer. In a soft whisper she confided, "She haunts this building, every day and every night. I once saw her upstairs climbing back into the grandfather clock. The one in the hall, across from the auditorium entrance."

"The grandfather clock upstairs?" Leah repeated in a halting voice. She swallowed hard and began to shiver.

"Uh, Pam—"

"Yes, Leah?"

"Let's get out of here." Without waiting for Pam's response, Leah turned on her heel and bolted out of the costume closet. She grabbed her bag and quickly tossed her tutu back into the wicker basket. Mrs. Slavinska could hang it up later. Pam followed close behind as Leah hurried into the hall. She had to get her coat out of her locker, but her fingers were trembling and she flubbed the combination three times.

"Here, let me," Pam said.

Leah nodded and whispered the combination for Pam, who opened it on the first try. Leah yanked her blue woolen jacket off the hook and turned to Pam. "Are you going home now?"

"I can't. But I'll see you later."

"Okay—bye," Leah squeaked. In the upstairs

hall she tiptoed past the grandfather clock with her eyes squeezed shut. Then she ran down the long hall and threw open the mansion's heavy front door. Brilliant sunlight blinded her, and for a moment Leah was totally disoriented. Pamela's story had made her feel as if it were midnight and all dark outside. But it wasn't night at all; it was the middle of a sunny Saturday afternoon, a clear blue December day. A group of little girls from Saturday's class for children pushed by Leah and scampered down the broad front steps. One of them stayed behind and looked up at Leah with saucerlike eyes.

"Are you a ballerina?" the little girl asked.

Leah bent down and hugged her and started to laugh. Whatever Pam had seen, there were no such things as ghosts. Pam just had an overactive imagination. The little girl was still staring at Leah, waiting for an answer. Leah kissed her rosy cheek and pulled the girl's woolen cap farther down over her long braids. "No, not yet. I study here, just like you. But someday—"

"Someday I'll be a ballerina, too!" the little girl cried, running off to join her friends.

Chapter 6

That night Leah flicked on her bedroom light and cried, "Misha, what are you doing?" The red-striped kitten was stretched out on the pale chenille bedspread purring so loudly Leah could hear him from the door. He returned her stare with adoring gold eyes, then got up, arched his back, and leapt off the bed.

"Misha?" Leah questioned, almost expecting the cat to answer. He rubbed against Leah's leg, then trotted back to the bed and jumped back up. He sat up straight with his white paws pressed neatly together and purred even louder. Leah approached the bed cautiously. There was something gray and fuzzy right in the middle of her pillow. "A mouse?" she said, her lips curling with distaste. Misha prowled across the bed to her side and brushed against her hand. "A mouse." Leah forced herself to repeat the word as neutrally as possible. "You caught a mouse and you gave it to me as a present. Good cat. Misha, you're a good cat."

Leah hoped Misha didn't think her congratulations were too halfhearted, but two mice in one day were a bit much. Leah was on her way to the hall to ask Mrs. Hanson what to do about Misha's catch, when she stopped dead in her tracks. She turned around, rushed back to the kitten and picked him up. "You caught a mouse, Misha, and you brought it to me. Now I have just the proof I need. Alex!" she shouted. "Alex, come here right away. I have something to show you."

A door slammed shut on the floor below, then Leah heard Alex's familiar quick step on the stairs. "What is happening? Is something wrong?" Alex asked.

Leah shook her head. She pointed to her bed. "Look what Misha brought me."

"Ugh!" Alex held her nose.

"Come off it, Sorokin, it doesn't smell. I think it's a perfectly fresh mouse and Misha brought it to me. Now, I was right, wasn't I?"

Alex wrapped her robe more tightly around her and kept her distance from the bed. "Just get rid of it, please," she begged.

Leah stood her ground. "Not until you agree. This is proof positive that Pamela Hunter hasn't been killing any mice lately. Never mind stuffing them into my shoes."

Alex wrinkled her brow. "I am not sure this is proof, but you do have a point." She finally smiled. "I think maybe Misha must have to do with the mouse." She paused, then turned to Leah with a little shiver. "Will you please get rid of it now."

"How?" Leah asked, sounding very uncertain.

"We could call Katrina!" Abby poked her head in the door. Abby shared the third floor of Mrs. Hanson's boardinghouse with Leah. "It is a very nasty thing to have on your bed."

"Calling Katrina is ridiculous," Alex pronounced. "I will get Mrs. Hanson."

"Why do you need Mrs. Hanson?" Pam poked her head over Alex's shoulder. "Another mouse?" She sounded shocked. "Where did it come from?"

"You should know!" Alex retorted.

"And what's that supposed to mean?" Pam snapped.

"Don't you remember, in class today you were the one who suggested Misha had put that mouse in Leah's toe shoe," Abby explained.

"Oh, yes. Silly me, forgetting all about my pretty little Misha like that." As if he were under a spell, the red cat jumped down from the bed and leapt into Pam's outstretched arms.

Leah felt an unreasonable pang of jealousy. She had brought Misha to the boardinghouse a couple of months before. Her very own kitten, she had raised him from when he was just a fistful of fluff. Misha had taken one look at Pam and fallen in love. Leah couldn't think of any other explanation for Misha's behavior. Kay had quipped that it was only because their hair was the same color. Most nights Misha slept downstairs in Pam's bedroom, though now and again he did seem to remember that he belonged to Leah. Once or twice a week at most he'd trot upstairs and deign to share Leah's pillow for the evening.

Downstairs the phone rang, and a moment later Mrs. Hanson called up, "Leah, it's for you! It's Chrissy."

"Oh—I'll be right there," Leah cried, then turned around and looked at the mouse still lying in the center of her bed. "Maybe I'd better dispose of this first."

"Don't worry. Your friend's calling long distance. I'll get rid of it." Pam put the cat down and headed toward the bed. Leah watched her, wondering why Pam was the one who wanted to do her such a big favor. "Go ahead. Mice don't scare me either. Katrina's not the only brave girl around here."

"Thanks, Pam—I owe you one," Leah tossed over her shoulder, then bolted down the stairs to the front hall two at a time.

"Chrissy Morely," Leah scolded, putting the phone to her ear. "Where have you been?"

"Where have *I* been?" Chrissy asked, horrified. "You're the one who's dropped out of sight, flown to Pluto, or else been kidnapped by the Bolshoi to be held hostage and displayed on Soviet television as America's great young ballet star."

"What are you talking about?" Leah said with a frown. She slid her back down the wall and sat on the floor. "I haven't gotten a letter from you in weeks and weeks and weeks—" Leah paused and corrected herself with a giggle. "At least not in two weeks."

"I wrote you twice last week and once the week before, and you haven't called, you haven't written—"

"But I didn't get any letters from you," Leah said, genuinely puzzled. Sometimes her mail from San Lorenzo was late, but it always turned up sooner or later. She looked up and saw Pam coming down the broad front stairs. The redhead held the mouse at arm's length by its tail. Misha trotted behind her, mewing loudly. She gave Leah a little three-fingered wave, then walked right down the hall to the back door, opened it a crack, and hurled Misha's catch out into the wilds of the yard. Misha yowled in protest, but Pam simply scooped him up and carried him off to her room.

"Leah, are you listening to me?" Chrissy sounded irritated.

"Uh—no—I wasn't. Sorry. Someone walked by with a mouse and—well, it's a long story. What's up with you?"

Chrissy quickly began to fill Leah in on the news. "The big scoop, of course, is Annie Mac-Phearson."

Leah's stomach tightened at the mention of Annie's name. Annie was a year older than Leah and had also been a student at Hannah Greene's school. She was currently an apprentice with the New York City Ballet and had been since she was Leah's age. Leah always felt vaguely competitive with Annie, as if the older girl had her foot more firmly planted on the road to a successful dance career.

"She's having a ballet choreographed on her!" Chrissy said, excited. "Now, I know that makes you jealous, but guess who she's dancing with."

Leah put her hands over her eyes. "Peter Martins!"

"Right. I heard it from Hannah the Banana herself. I ran into her at Sneaky Pete's. She sends you her love."

Leah had no idea what to say, so she sat there silent a minute. Finally Chrissy called into the phone, "Stephenson, earth to Stephenson!"

"I'm here, Chrissy. I must admit I'm writhing with envy. Wait until you hear what's been happening with me."

Leah told Chrissy all about the Louise Adams Scholarship and how she hadn't gotten the lead in *Swan Lake*.

"That's rotten," Chrissy said at the end of the story. "But at least your friend Katrina didn't have to leave the school. Whatever happened to that awful Pamela Hunter? Has she broken both her legs yet? Anything suitable like that?"

Chrissy's question took Leah totally by surprise. She had forgotten how much she had confided in her best friend when Pam had given her trouble during entrance auditions. She wanted to tell Chrissy how her feelings toward Pam were changing, but just then she looked up. Pam's bedroom was a converted sun porch that opened out from the living room. From Leah's perch in the hall she could see through the arched entrance to the parlor and past the piano to Pamela's door. Pam's room was already dark. Leah figured she was already asleep, with Misha at her side. It would be safe to talk about her change of heart to Chrissy. Chrissy was a sensible, fair person who wasn't involved in Pam's past history at all, and Leah sure could use some objective advice on the subject.

Leah cleared her throat and prepared to lower her voice, when she caught a glimpse of something moving out of the corner of her eye. Leah's shoulders tightened, and she whipped her head around, just in time to see the lacy sleeve of a cream-colored robe and a mop of red hair slip out of sight behind the living room door. Leah couldn't believe it: Pamela Hunter was up to her old tricks again—eavesdropping, like she had done at least ten times before, on Leah's private conversation. Pam had heard everything Leah had just confided to Chrissy: how she felt about Katrina, how depressed she was about not getting the lead role, how insecure Leah had been feeling about her dancing and her whole future as a ballerina. Leah was mad, and also humiliated. When she told Kay that she certainly wouldn't trust Pam enough to show her the private jottings in her journal, she had been dead serious. And some of what she had told Chrissy right now she hadn't even confided to the pages of her notebook.

Leah's first impulse was to slam down the phone, march up to Pam, and accuse her there and then. But something stopped Leah. Accuse Pam of what? Of being in the living room while Leah was on the phone? The living room was an area all the girls used. Pam had every right to be in the living room, even with the lights off, when Leah was on the phone. Leah thought Pam had been spying on her, but she felt obliged to give Pam a chance to prove herself innocent. Flying off the handle didn't seem the right way to go about finding out what the real Pam Hunter was like.

"Leah, are you still there?" Chrissy shouted into the phone.

"Listen, I've got heaps more to tell you, Chrissy, but I'll write you a nice long letter tomorrow, okay?"

"Ah," Chrissy said knowingly. "The line—as they say in Washington—is not secure."

Leah had to laugh. She promised to write Chrissy soon, then hung up the phone. She sat back on her heels and wondered what to do next. She could confront Pam now, wait until tomorrow, or just let the whole thing drop. Waiting wasn't something Leah did very well, and pretending she hadn't seen Pam wouldn't work. Leah was a terrible liar. She had to confront Pam.

Leah got up and went into the living room. "Pam," she called in a soft voice. No one answered. The door to Pam's room was shut, just like before. The clock on the mantel ticked loudly. From upstairs Leah could hear the subdued beat of Kay and Linda's stereo, and voices from Suzanne's portable TV. Leah bit her lip and tried again. "Pam, I need to talk to you. It's important."

"Leah, is that you?" a sleepy voice replied. "Is something wrong? I was asleep, but if you need me, I'll get up."

Leah closed her eyes and counted to ten. Yes, plenty is wrong, Pamela Hunter, she replied inwardly. But aloud she said, "Never mind, Pam. It can wait until tomorrow morning." Leah was too tired to get into an argument with Pam now. Pretending she had been sleeping while Leah was on the phone was a typical underhanded Pam move. Leah shoved her hair out of her face and flashed a dirty look in the general direction of Pam's room. She climbed upstairs thinking by morning she might not even be interested in what "the real Pam Hunter" had to say for herself.

"I know exactly why you're angry with me," Pam told Leah. Mr. Robson had ordered his dancers to take a break while he argued the fine points of Kenny's solo with the company dance notator. They had been discussing it for ten minutes now, and Leah sat on the floor massaging a tight spot in her left calf. If Robson didn't get them dancing again soon, they'd all have a case of terminally cold muscles. Somehow Leah had a feeling that Christopher Robson wasn't going to give them a chance to go through warm-ups again before going through the routine. She was tired and irritable, and Mr. Robson had been on her case all afternoon.

Leah felt as if she were going to explode, and she was definitely not in the mood to deal with Pam. Leah had managed not to talk to her all day so far, and she was about to tell Pam to get lost, when Pam stopped her battements at the barre and dropped down onto the floor at Leah's side.

"And Leah, I don't blame you one bit. Why, I wouldn't speak to me either. Not at all."

"Don't flatter yourself, Pam," Kenny said brusquely. He was lying on the floor in a shoulder stand, stretching out his back and legs. He held them straight up for a moment, then eased them down with his toes brushing the floor behind his head. "Leah's angry at Robson, not you." Leah took a deep breath. She scrambled to her feet and walked away from Kenny and Pam. Putting one hand on the barre, she began to do her warm-up pliés all over again.

Pam stood up, too. She put her opposite hand on the barre and faced Leah. "I know you saw me last night. I was listening to your conversation with your friend. I shouldn't have done that. I'm sorry."

Leah was halfway down in a grand plié when Pam said that. She straightened up quickly and shoved the sleeves of her blue cardigan up on her arms. "Did I hear that right? Did you just admit that you were eavesdropping on my conversation?"

Pam looked down at the floor and studied her feet. "Yes." She looked up and her green eyes were wide and innocent-looking. "I apologize. I shouldn't have done that."

"Listen, Pam," Leah began, for the life of her unable to fathom what was going on in Pam's head, "if you shouldn't have done it, why did you?"

"I—I couldn't help myself." Pam tugged down the back of her leotard and began practicing a series of battements tendu. The sharp, strong movement of her foot as she pointed it out first in front of her, then to the side and to the back, contrasted harshly with her shy, humble expression.

"Pamela Hunter, I don't believe you."

"But it's true—I couldn't." Pam looked quickly at Kenny, then lowered her voice so only Leah could hear. "Don't you understand?" she said, and placed an urgent hand on Leah's arm. "I know it's awful, but as long as I remember, people haven't liked me very much. My mother says they're jealous. I guess I'm a strong dancer and I'm attractive—"

Leah's blue eyes narrowed as she tried to figure out Pam. On the one hand, Pam was admitting she'd done wrong, but on the other, she was trying to excuse her behavior on the grounds that people were jealous of her good looks and talent. A warning bell went off in Leah's head, but she wanted to hear Pam out. The redhead's admission of guilt had taken Leah offguard, but perhaps this was Pam's way of trying to be friends.

"I know how stuck-up that all sounds, but you know how people are sometimes. They get jealous about the darnedest things. Anyway, I got this nasty habit, and it's so hard to shake. I can't help but want to listen to see if people are talking about me and—" Pam broke off and bit her lip, and Leah detected the glint of tears in Pam's cool green eyes.

"So you listened to me to see if I was going to talk about you to my best friend back home," Leah finished for her in a quiet, flat voice. She took a deep breath and found herself smiling—it was a small smile, but it was enough to reassure Pam. Pam nodded and smiled back, too.

Leah cleared her throat. "Pam, if you want people to be your friends, you have to trust them. I might have said something to Chrissy about you last night. Would hearing me say it—whether it was bad or good—make you really feel any better about me or about yourself?"

Slowly Pam shook her head back and forth. For the second time in two days she reminded Leah of a little girl. "I hadn't thought of it that way. I just wanted to know what people were saying about me so I'd know how to defend myself."

"But if you didn't do things like eavesdrop," Leah said sharply, "you wouldn't have to defend yourself in the first place."

"Oh, Leah." Pam folded her hands in a pretty pleading gesture—the same one she had used with Madame the day before. "I never thought of it like that. I promise, I'll never ever eavesdrop on you—" Pam covered her mouth and let out a cute giggle. "I mean, on *anyone* again!"

"Places!" Christopher roared. Pam and Leah both jumped a little at the sound of his voice. Leah yanked off her leg warmers and started to her spot behind the strip of masking tape that marked the wings.

"Psssst!"

Leah turned around ever so slightly and cast a questioning glance in Pam's direction.

"Friends?" Pam asked in a stage whisper.

Kenny whipped around and glared at her. He made a sound of disgust and shook his head.

Leah ignored Kenny and whispered back to Pam, "Friends."

For the first few minutes after the break, Christopher was too preoccupied with his argument with the dance notator to bother Leah much. She let herself relax, allowing the music to take over, to move her through the steps. She stopped thinking so consciously about her position onstage, her technique. She glided behind Kenny and posed in a low, pretty arabesque, then bouréed in front of him to prepare for a supported pirouette. His hands closed around her small waist as Leah went into her preparation. She focused her eyes on a spot on the wall behind Robert's head and sprang into her turn.

Kenny stopped her neatly after her second time around, and Leah began her preparation for the next enchaînement.

"Beautiful!" Kenny murmured, and reached his left hand out to begin a sequence of steps with Pam.

"Disgusting!" Christopher shouted, and rapped his yardstick loudly on the piano. Robert stopped the music, and Leah and Pam both stared at the coach.

"What did I do now?" Pamela snapped.

Christopher didn't acknowledge Pam's question. He looked right past her as if she didn't even exist. "Miss Stephenson—like I told you the other day, pride always comes before a fall. Always!" He rammed his fist down hard on the piano, sending Robert's sheet music flying in all directions. Robert pursed his lips, then quietly got up and began retrieving the music.

Leah's whole body stiffened. She clenched her fists and dug her nails into her palms. Why was he picking on her today? Leah took a couple of quick deep breaths and tried to calm down. If Christopher didn't leave her alone soon, she was going to explode.

"Don't look at me that way, Stephenson!" he barked, and tried to stare her down. Leah refused to lower her eyes, and the pink in her cheeks deepened.

"Your little performance just now was very

clumsy. I didn't really expect to be coaching the jolly green giant through a pas de trois this afternoon. I expected to be coaching a supposedly talented scholarship student, the kind of young dancer that people say belongs at SFBA." He turned his back on Leah and strutted over to the piano.

Leah caught Pam's eye in the mirror. Pam flashed her a sympathetic smile. Leah did not smile back. She felt like walking up to Mr. Robson and slapping him on the face. Leah wasn't a violent person—she even hated killing insects. But she was getting sick of sitting back and taking so much verbal abuse from her teacher. At the moment the only thing in the world she was absolutely sure of was that she hated dancing in front of Christopher Robson and never wanted to dance a single step for him again.

Robson spun around on his heel and glared at her, tapping his lips with the tip of his finger. "In fact," he said coolly, "now that I've had the opportunity to work so closely with you, I can't imagine how you ever got accepted to this Academy in the first place."

"Oh, shut up!" Leah stamped her foot so hard it hurt. The teacher's pale eyebrows arched up above the rim of his glasses. Leah stomped right up to him. "In case you don't remember, Mr. Robson, you were one of the judges who let me into this dumb school. You were the person who decided I deserved the Golden Gate Award. You could have given it to any of the other first-year girls in this room. But you didn't. So if any mistake's been made, it's your fault. Not mine." Leah cast one last scathing glance in Robson's direction, then she turned on her heel and paraded over to the piano. She yanked her dance bag out from under it and hoisted it up to her shoulder. Without a backward glance she started for the dressing room door. "Now it's your turn!" she said bitterly to Abby.

"Stop!" Mr. Robson's voice boomed across the West Studio. "Leah, come back here."

Leah stood her ground, though her knees started shaking. Suddenly she was very afraid: what had she just done? One big outburst of temper and she had thrown her life's dream down the drain. Visions of a desolate future passed quickly before her eyes, a future with no SFBA in it ... a future without dancing.

"I'm sorry, Leah."

Leah turned around and found herself staring right at Christopher. He peered at her over the rims of his glasses. "I'm sorry, but I had to do that!"

Leah's forehead creased in a suspicious frown. He *had* to insult her every afternoon? She averted her eyes and looked at the dressing room door, still furious.

"You are a good dancer," he said, and Leah could hardly believe her ears. He didn't even sound sarcastic. "But you are too lyrical. You don't perform with enough passion. Now at least I know you can give a passionate performance."

Leah turned to face him again, humiliated. "You were playing with my head!" she cried.

"Sometimes teachers have to do that."

Leah took a deep breath. "So, does that mean you want me to go on?"

"Yes."

Leah tossed her bag down under the barre and walked with her back held very straight over to Kenny. "Sorry about that," she said to him and

Pam. She wasn't sorry she had yelled at Christopher, however. No matter what his motives were, he deserved whatever Leah had said to him.

Kenny smiled at Leah and took her hand. He walked Leah back over to their starting position.

"As for you, Hunter," Christopher said over his shoulder, "I want you at least two or three pounds thinner by Thursday. You're gaining weight, and it's affecting your dancing."

Leah winced and looked quickly at Pam. The redhead's lips were pursed tightly shut, and her strong chin was tilted up in the air. "My costume fits perfectly, Mr. Robson. I have not gained an ounce since I've come here."

"The costume may fit, dearie," Christopher said in a cutting voice, "but the steps don't. So shape up!"

The music started and Leah whispered quickly under her breath, "Pam, it's just his way. He has to pick on someone."

Pam didn't answer. She stared straight ahead, and when the threesome began their dance, Leah could hear the heavy thud of Pam's feet as she angrily attacked each step.

Chapter 7

"*Pam, you are not fat!*" Leah said the minute the girls hit the dressing room. Robson had been devastating today, and though Leah had scored some kind of minor victory over the teacher, she was even more convinced that he was the meanest person she'd ever met.

With a proud toss of her head Pamela answered, "No, of course I'm not. It is perfectly obvious that man just needs new glasses."

Abby giggled. "That's a good one, Pam. I hadn't thought of that." She turned to Leah, and her small hazel eyes glowed with respect. "You really put him in his place, Leah."

Leah nodded. "It felt good, too. I wish I could have blown up sooner—it would have done me some good."

"You could say that again!" Pam muttered.

Leah wasn't sure she'd heard right. "What did you say?"

"Oh, only that if you had spoken up sooner, maybe he would have stopped picking on you. I do declare," Pam said, letting down her thick hair and running her fingers through it. She had pulled off her tights and leotard and tossed them on a nearby chair. "You certainly have spirit, Leah. You impressed him, you know."

Leah wasn't so sure about that. "Tomorrow he'll be laying into me again. I'd bet my life on it."

"You know who'll really be laying into us," Mia warned from a stool by the door. "Madame. It's full cast call for the third act this afternoon, and we're all already twenty minutes late."

"Oh, no!" Leah wailed, and flopped back in her chair. She had one leg of her tights on and one leg off. "I forgot all about that rehearsal. I can't dance another step. I just can't!"

"Can't," Mia said with a knowing smile, "is one word that is definitely not in Madame's vocabulary." She yanked a longish full skirt over her leotard and pulled a pair of low-heeled leather shoes out of a cubbyhole. After a quick combing of her neatly groomed dark hair, Mia was on her way out the door. "I'll mention rehearsal ran late, but you all better hurry up."

"Hurry up?" Leah said. She stared blankly at her tights and proceeded to put them back on. "If I had one million dollars and a date to dance with Baryshnikov in New York, I'd pass it all up just for a hot bath, some lunch, and a chance to rest my poor feet."

"Wouldn't we all!" Pam said curtly. "But you heard Mia."

"I'm ready!" Abby announced. She fingered the beige fabric of the skirt she used for character dancing class, and waited to see if Pam and Leah would go downstairs with her to the Green Studio.

Pam replied with a wave of her hand. "Abigail, why don't you all run down. We'll be along in a second. I can't seem to find my boots. You know, Leah, the red ones we use for 'the mazurka.'"

Leah yanked her skirt over her head and fiddled with the tricky button at the waist. "Uh—I haven't seen your boots, Pam." Leah had already put hers on. They were red and soft, and Leah wished she could have a pair just like them with heavier soles for streetwear. She looked at Pam. "Pam, you have your street clothes on!"

"My what—" Pam glanced down in surprise at her tight leather pants, her loose silky shirt, and her tiny black ankle boots. "Oh, Leah, I'm going right out of my mind." She stared ruefully at the balled-up leotard and tights she'd flung on a chair. "I've got to put my sweaty clothes back on." Pam quickly unbuttoned her blouse and slipped out of her pants. "Do you think Madame will let me wear *these* boots?" she asked, a note of hope in her voice.

Leah shook her head. "You know the rule, no street shoes in the classroom." Leah jabbed some hairpins into her bun and checked her reflection in the mirror. Then she headed for the door.

"Wait, Leah! I just remembered. I had my mazurka boots downstairs yesterday, in the wardrobe. They were a little too tight and I asked Mrs. Slavinska to stretch them. I guess I forgot to bring them up."

"I'll tell Madame you'll be only a little late then," Leah assured Pam with a smile.

"Leah, can you do me a favor?" Pam grabbed Leah's arm. "Please? I'll be another six or seven minutes at least getting myself ready, and then I have to go all the way to the basement—Madame is always harder on me than she is on you. If you're a few minutes late, she won't have a fit. Could you—"

"Go to the wardrobe room for you?" Leah finished the sentence for her. She looked at Pam. It would be more like ten minutes before she got her hair up again and her practice clothes back on. "Okay, I'll do it. But you owe me one!" Leah reminded her.

"Oh, yes, Leah. I'll keep that in mind. I do owe you one!"

Leah ran down the back stairs at record speed. She jumped over the last couple of steps and jogged down the deserted hall. Sundays at the Academy always felt a little strange to Leah. Most of the dancers in the company and school turned up for morning class, but afterward the place more or less emptied out. Of course someone was always rehearsing upstairs, but the cafeteria in the basement was closed. Leah skidded to a stop in front of the wardrobe room and stared blankly at the closed door. "What if it's locked!" she said aloud, and felt vaguely annoyed Pam hadn't thought of that possibility. With a sinking feeling in her stomach Leah put her hand on the doorknob. To her surprise it opened easily.

The door creaked on its hinges, and a vague sense of fear shot through Leah. Leah reached into the room and groped for the light switch on the wall. Finally her fingers made out the shape of the switch and she flicked the overheads on. The air in the room was close and stuffy, and Leah understood now why Mrs. Slavinska was always complaining about the basement workroom. Leah made her way quickly through the obstacle course of sewing machines and storage trunks to the closet door. It was ajar; the red glow of a safety light on the closet's back wall cast eerie shadows on the racks of costumes.

Leah poked her head in and looked around. The light was dim, and at first glance Leah didn't see Pam's mazurka boots. "Next time that girl runs her own errands," Leah grumbled. She noticed a chain hanging from the fixture on the low closet ceiling. She pulled it and a 25-watt bulb brightened the storage room. Leah frowned. Mrs. Slavinsky had probably put Pam's boots with the other character shoes. Leah looked around and finally spotted a row of boots peeking out from beneath some capes. She stooped down to see if Pam's were there.

Suddenly there was a loud banging noise, and Leah jumped.

"Oh, no!" she wailed. "The door!" In two long strides Leah was over by the closet door. She pushed against it as hard as she could with her body, but it didn't budge. With a nervous laugh she tried the handle. It turned, but the door still didn't open. She pushed and shoved, then rattled the handle some more, but the door didn't move. The door had a lock to it, and something, a vibration from the floor above, or maybe a gust of wind, had blown it shut. It had locked automatically. Leah wanted to kick herself. She wasn't sure she could have prevented the accident, but if she had known the door had a lock on it, she would have propped it open with something before wandering into the closet.

"What do I do now?" she cried, and felt a panicky sensation in her chest. Leah hated being alone in closed small places and had never been very fond of basements. Back home her mother practically had to bribe her with the promise of dessert to get her to fetch frozen food from the basement freezer.

Leah forced herself to stay calm. Getting hysterical was not going to get her out of this mess. She sat back on her heels and fingered the bright ribbon trim on the hem of her skirt. She gulped down a couple of deep breaths of air and forced herself to relax. Slowly the frantic beating of her heart quieted down, and she began to think more clearly. She looked around the crowded closet and tried to see if there was a window leading out into the hall, or a door. She got up, and, avoiding Letitia's eyes in the photograph on the wall, walked to the back of the wall. Maybe if there was a safety light, there was some kind of fire exit. Leah pushed aside the fur capes and long trailing gowns, but there was no door—only the dim red light.

She sank back against the comforting fur of the capes and sighed with frustration. "How will I ever get out of here?" she whispered. Leah had no idea how long she stood there with her arms folded across her chest, sick with worry and with no idea what to do next. Madame would be furious with her, she was sure of that. After the little lecture in class about nothing, absolutely nothing, keeping a dancer from dancing, Madame was going to give Leah an earful after missing today's rehearsal. It was one of only two full cast rehearsals scheduled before Tuesday's dress rehearsal.

"The rehearsal!" Leah suddenly straightened up and marched back to the door. Pam was at the rehearsal! She knew where Leah had gone, and when Leah didn't turn up, she would tell Madame what had happened and someone would come looking for her. Leah took hope from that and began pounding the door and yelling. "Help! Let me out of here. I'm in the closet. Help!" she shouted. But no one came to rescue her. Finally Leah's fists started hurting, and her voice became hoarse. Tears of frustration welled up in her eyes. She stuffed her sore hands into the roomy pockets of her skirt, and her fingers closed around her watch.

Leah pulled it out. When she looked at the time she practically fainted. She had been stuck for over an hour, and rehearsal was probably halfway over. Why hadn't Pam sent someone to find her? Her boots were probably back at the boarding-house and not even in this building at all. Leah felt as if she could strangle Pam. Being stuck here was all her fault.

Leah looked at her watch again and had a terrible thought: it was Sunday afternoon and already past five o'clock. Why should anyone come down to the basement? The cafeteria was closed, and no academic classes were in session. Leah shuddered at her next thought—she could be stuck in the closet all night. "What am I thinking of," Leah said. The sound of her own voice made her feel a little better. "Pam will send someone soon. I'm sure she will. I'll just wait." Leah closed her eyes and tried to figure out why Pam hadn't send anyone yet. She must have told somebody— unless—Leah's eyes snapped open—unless Pam decided to skip rehearsal entirely! The possibility wasn't beyond Pam—she had done that very thing the afternoon before. Pam had probably just gone home. And no one at rehearsal would have known where either she or Leah had gone. Certainly no one in the building would think of looking for Leah here, in the closet in the wardrobe room. In fact, no one would even know she was missing.

Leah shrank back in horror against the clothes rack and contemplated her fate. Her bottom lip began to tremble, and the tears she had held back in the last hour started streaming from her eyes. She sobbed uncontrollably for a few minutes, then shook her head. Crying wouldn't solve a thing. It wouldn't make the time pass faster or stop the rumbling of her empty stomach. "That's the last time I skip lunch!" Leah said aloud.

Leah decided to make herself comfortable. She selected a fake ermine cape from the rack and shrugged it around her slender shoulders, then sat back down on the floor and tucked her feet under its folds. Her red mazurka boots were snug, and she pulled them off. She wriggled her toes to get the circulation started again and tried to figure out how to pass the time. The air in the closet was even closer than in the wardrobe room itself, but as the hour grew later, dampness crept in through the cellar walls, and Leah grew cold. She pulled the thick furry collar close to her face and closed her eyes. In a few minutes she drifted into a light sleep.

Something made her eyes flutter open, and Leah couldn't tell at first if she was dreaming. Above her head the single small light bulb flickered, and Leah watched with dismay as shadows danced wildly on the closet floor and walls. Leah blinked and rubbed her eyes with her fists. She couldn't tell if she had been sleeping for a few minutes or for hours. She pinched herself hard to make sure she was awake and grunted with pain. All at once the vague tumble of thoughts in her head began to take shape. The light bulb was about to go out, and then Leah would be left in the closet in almost total darkness. She scrambled to her feet

and stared helplessly as the filament inside the
bulb began to sizzle. Leah's eyes shifted from the
ceiling to the opposite wall, to the oval-framed
photo above the dresser. In the flickering light it
seemed Letitia Moorehouse was laughing at her.
Leah's hand stole to her throat, and she began to
shake. Pam's tale of poor Letty was still fresh in
Leah's mind. She had tried hard not to think
about it, but the fear of meeting up with Letty's
ghost had been somewhere in Leah's heart ever
since she set foot in the closet. Yesterday in the
sunlight and beneath the clear blue sky, Pam's
story about Letitia's ghost had seemed silly, the
kind of story you told over a campfire or at a
slumber party but that had no truth to it. But
alone in the near dark, Letty Moorehouse's ghost
seemed all too real. Leah's throat went dry.

Keeping her back pressed against the wall of
costumes, Leah edged her way to the door, her
glance held captive by Letitia's soulful eyes. Leah
heard a sudden "pop" and the closet went dark—
except for the tiny red safety light. The terrible
prospect of being locked up in a closet with the
ghost of a woman gone mad from a broken heart
sent a surge of energy through Leah's slight body.
Not caring anymore if Letitia's eyes were staring
at her, Leah pummeled the closet door with her
hands and kicked it with her feet. When her hands
got tired, she groped in the dark for her dance
bag and pulled out her toe shoes. They were new
shoes, and later she would regret ruining them,
but at the moment she didn't have any choice.
She hammered the door with her shoes. She was
too scared to scream. When she opened her mouth,
the words wouldn't come out.

All at once Leah heard the shuffle of footsteps

out in the basement corridor. Leah's lips parted
in a smile, and she scrubbed the sleeve of her
leotard across her face and tried to find her voice.
then from somewhere behind her she heard a low
wail.

"Leeeaah ... Leeeaah ..."

Leah bit the back of her hand, trying to stifle
the urge to scream. If she were quiet enough, the
ghost might not be able to find her. Her eyes
searched the semidarkness of the closet. The
Academy building was really haunted—Pam had
told the truth. Letitia lived in the grandfather
clock in the upstairs hall by day, but by night ...

Leah heard her name again, and another shuffle of feet. She closed her eyes and put her hands
over her ears, but the shuffles grew louder and
louder. She heard the footsteps pause outside the
wardrobe room and then the creak of the door.

Leah jumped back from the closet entrance
just in time. The door flew open, and Leah let out
the terrified scream that had been building up
inside her for the last few hours.

Chapter 8

"Leah! What happened?" A pair of strong arms enveloped Leah, and she recognized the voice of Raul Zamora, the Academy's fencing and drama teacher. Raul was also the director of San Francisco's Teatro Hispánico.

Leah looked up into Raul's dark eyes. A sense of relief overwhelmed Leah, and she clutched Raul more tightly. "You're real! You're not a ghost!" The words spilled out of Leah, followed by a sob, and then another and another. A wave of exhaustion washed over Leah, and she collapsed in Raul's arms, weeping. Then Kenny was beside her, helping her out of the closet and into the brightly lit wardrobe room. He helped her sit down on one of the costume trunks.

Leah cried into her hands and gratefully accepted the clean white handkerchief Raul offered her. She caught sight of Madame Preston through the blue of her tears. Madame was standing in the doorway. The older woman's face was creased with concern. Before Leah could think about what she was doing, she stood up and flew across the room into Madame's arms.

"Now, now, dear." Madame's hands were surprisingly gentle as she smoothed back the hair from Leah's forehead. She hugged Leah warmly and said in a soft voice, "Everything's all right now. We found you." Madame's warmth came as such a surprise to Leah that her tears fell faster. But slowly, as her sobs died down, the reality of the situation dawned on Leah: Madame had been worried enough about Leah to join a search for her.

Leah pulled away from Madame Preston's embrace. "Oh, Madame. I'm so sorry I caused you all this trouble." She twisted Raul's handkerchief nervously in her hands but forced herself to meet Madame's stern gray eyes.

The director was looking right down at Leah with a puzzled frown on her face. She shook her head and said quietly, "It's all right, Leah. I'm not going to punish you for this." She paused, then said firmly, "But I do expect some sort of explanation. How in the world did you get locked in the wardrobe closet in the first place?" Madame seemed to notice Leah's clothes for the first time. "You're wearing your character skirt—were you on your way to rehearsal?"

"Yes—" Leah paused. She needed time to think, to clear her head. Whatever she said, she didn't want to get Pam in trouble for sending her down to the basement. After all, she could have said no to Pam. And if she had been smart, that's exactly what she would have done. "It's my own fault I missed rehearsal," Leah said bravely, then shook her head. "But I didn't lock myself in the closet. The wind did that."

"The wind?" Kenny sounded incredulous. "What wind?" He fanned his face with his hand as if to say that that was the only breeze in the room. It was true—there was no wind in the basement, which is why the air was always so stale, Leah reflected. "Leah, can I get you anything from the vending machine?" Kenny asked. He looked surprised when Madame told him to get a soda and something to eat for Leah, but strolled off toward the machine.

"I can't say I've ever felt a draft down here myself," Raul mused.

A creepy sensation ran down Leah's spine. If wind hadn't blown the closet door shut, what had?

"Leah, I don't think I have to remind you that the wardrobe room is off limits to students unless Mrs. Slavinska or one of her assistants is down here." She paused and toyed with the silver and coral ring she wore on her right hand. Just before she started to speak again, Leah thought she detected the faintest trace of a smile on Madame's thin lips. "I am sure that is one rule I will never have to remind *you* of again." She looked up at Leah, her face serious but her eyes laughing.

Leah couldn't help but return a small, sheepish smile.

Madame cleared her throat. "But you didn't quite answer my question, Leah. What in the world possessed you to get dressed for rehearsal and come down here? I thought you had a coaching session earlier this afternoon with Mr. Robson. When I phoned him this evening, he said all three casts left a little late, but that as far as he knew, you were on your way to the Green Studio."

"I came down to look for Pam's mazurka boots—"

Madame looked confused, but it was Kenny who spoke up first. He had just returned from the vending machine, and he opened a can of diet soda for Leah and handed her a packet of cheese and peanut butter crackers. "What are you talking about? Pam had her boots in class. She was wearing them." He let out a sharp, annoyed laugh. "I should know."

Leah stared at Kenny and shook her head in disbelief. "I don't get it. She told me she couldn't find them and that she had probably left them down here. If she found them for class, then why didn't she tell someone where I was? Why did she leave me alone down here for so long?" Leah's voice rose to a hysterical pitch.

"Because she thought you skipped rehearsal altogether and went right home," Madame calmly explained, sitting down on a chair next to Leah and smoothing a wrinkle out of her cream-colored pants.

It didn't make sense to Leah. She took a long drink of her soda. She had been in the closet almost five hours, and she was dying of thirst. Her dry throat felt better instantly, but the soda did nothing to solve the mystery of why Pam had made up that story. Leah set the can of soda down carefully and pushed her hair back from her temples. "Why would Pam say that?" she finally asked. "She knew where I was."

"Yes, I suppose she did," Madame said, as if she was just beginning to figure something out. "In fact, she did say you had gone to fetch her boots and that probably when you didn't find them, you decided it was too late to come to rehearsal anyway. She said you both had come to the same conclusion after fittings yesterday."

Alicia Preston's voice was neutral, and that surprised Leah. She suddenly felt a new respect for the school director. Madame obviously realized just how scared Leah had been, and she wasn't going to use the opportunity to lecture her or dole out some punishment like grounding her over the Christmas season, or something terrible like that. Madame always said that skipping rehearsal was something a budding ballerina would never do, no matter how dire the circumstances. Glad to be spared Madame's wrath, Leah relaxed a little and turned her attention back to the problem with Pam. Something about the whole incident, Pam sending her for the boots, then not telling Madame where she was, and worst of all, telling Madame about how they had both skipped rehearsal on purpose the afternoon before, really bothered Leah. And if Pam was indeed up to her old tricks, Leah was not going to sit back and be a willing victim. "I'm sorry, Madame, I don't know what ever gave Pam the idea I would skip rehearsal—"

"That doesn't matter now," Madame interrupted a little sharply. "Abigail and some of the other girls heard you say you were too tired to rehearse. I'm only sorry Pam didn't tell us exactly where you went to look for her boots." Madame drummed her fingers against the sewing table. "But the point is, you are fine."

"No, that's not the point," Leah said, contradicting Madame for the first time. "The point is, no one knew where to look for me for five hours, when Pam could—and should—have told you I had come down here."

"But Pam had no idea you were even missing," Madame informed Leah.

"I—I don't understand."

"Her parents arrived this afternoon. They picked Pam up at school right after class, so no one knew you were missing until after supper at the boardinghouse. I'm afraid, my dear, that this is one time we can't blame Pam for our problems," Madame said, her tone becoming increasingly colder.

"But what I don't get is how this closet ever locked in the first place," Raul said. He was crouched down in front of the door toying with the lock: the doorknob had a button that twisted on the outside to lock the door. "I don't understand it. Maybe there was a vibration from a truck outside or something. Well, it won't happen again!" Raul grabbed a roll of masking tape from the pattern table and taped over the button in the brass doorknob. Then he covered the brass plate on the side of the door so that the lock would never accidentally be triggered again.

Madame turned to Leah. "Leah, the point is not to blame anyone—including yourself—for what happened. You made a mistake coming down here alone and rummaging in the closet, but you had no way of knowing the door would lock behind you. Until now I never even suspected that closet *had* a lock. It seems like a rather silly precaution," she said with some energy, and Leah was sure that Mrs. Slavinska would hear more on the subject in the morning. Mrs. Slavinska had once told Leah that she was convinced thieves were going to break into her wardrobe room and steal the precious wigs and hats and bits of glittery fabric, and she was not going to relish having her closet unlocked.

Madame stood up, and Leah took this as a sign the round of questions was over. Kenny went into the closet and emerged with Leah's boots and her dance bag. Leah started for the door, but Madame put a restraining hand on her shoulder. "Leah, I have one more question." She moistened her lips, and Leah could see her struggling not to smile. "Why did you scream when Raul opened the door?"

Leah didn't know what to say. How could she possibly explain? She looked helplessly at Madame, but the director's gaze was steady. "I was afraid—" Leah started, and stared down at the floor. "I thought Raul was Letitia Moorehouse's ghost—coming to get me." Voicing her fears aloud really made them sound silly, and Leah felt her face grow scarlet with embarrassment.

There was a moment's stunned silence in the room, then Madame started laughing. "The ghost of Letitia Moorehouse?" she gasped, and sank back down on the chair. She threw her head back and laughed so hard, tears started down her cheeks.

Leah and Kenny traded glances. Wait until everyone hears about this! Leah thought, suddenly relishing the thought of going back to the boardinghouse and telling Alex and Kay that dignified, elegant Madame Preston had doubled over with giggles. It was a sight Leah was glad she hadn't missed.

Finally Madame recovered, pulled a tissue out of her bag, and with a graceful gesture dabbed at her tears of laughter. "Leah," Madame said, struggling to keep a straight face, "where in the world did you get the idea that Letitia Moorehouse was a ghost?"

"I—I heard it from—from someone." She wasn't about to bring up Pam's name again, not if she could help it. She explained about seeing the photograph in the wardrobe closet and how when she mentioned it to one of the girls she had heard the whole story. Then she recounted it, and usually hyperactive Kenny Rotolo stood stock-still, listening, spellbound.

Leah concluded by saying, "I heard the story recently, and then when the lights went off in the closet and I heard someone calling my name, I thought she had come to haunt me." Leah felt stupid admitting that, but then she saw Kenny nervously look back over his shoulder toward the open closet door, and she didn't feel quite so silly.

"Oh, Leah," Madame said, taking Leah's hand. "There is, I am sorry to tell you, no ghost."

"Oh, I'm not sorry at all!" Leah blurted out.

Madame bit her lip and looked down at her shoes. She brushed a speck of glitter off the fabric of her coat. "Letitia Moorehouse certainly existed, and her photograph is in the closet. It belongs upstairs in the auditorium, but until the renovations are finished, we wanted to store it in a safe place." Madame patted the chair next to her, and Leah sat down.

"I must say that is a very romantic story, and part of it *is* true. Letitia certainly was a young girl during the great earthquake, and she lived in this house—but with her husband and three children."

Leah's mouth formed a silent "oh."

"After the quake she and her husband had five more children, and she died only a few years ago, quite hale and hearty until the last few months before her death."

"But Pam told me—"

Kenny rolled his eyes to the ceiling. "I knew that girl was behind all this. Madame Preston," Kenny warned sharply, "I don't think any of this was an accident."

Leah jumped to Pam's defense. "That's unfair, Kenny, really."

"Leah's right," Madame agreed. "Pam might have told Leah this silly story, but I don't think you can blame Pam for Leah's being—well—so gullible." Madame softened her comment with a squeeze of Leah's hand.

"Maybe you're right," Kenny said grudgingly. "But that girl should learn to keep her mouth shut."

Raul picked up Leah's bag and motioned toward the door. "Don't be so hard on Pam, Kenny. I think she probably believed the story herself. That girl has a taste for the macabre!" Raul chuckled. "Every time I see her she has her nose buried in the latest thriller by Stephen King. She's one of those kids who loves spooky ghost stories. I used to, too." Raul led the small group out into the corridor and locked the wardrobe room door behind him.

"I do hope you will set Pamela straight about Letitia Moorehouse," Madame said as they started up the back stairs. "After all, it was the very same woman who bequeathed this mansion to the Bay Area Ballet and the Academy. Without dear Letitia there wouldn't be any wardrobe closet to haunt!"

"That is the wildest story I have ever heard!"

Alexandra told Leah an hour later across Mrs. Hanson's kitchen table. "But I have to agree with Kenny. It is so stuffy down in that basement, I cannot imagine the wind closing the door like that behind you. It does not make sense."

Alex leaned back in her seat as Mrs. Hanson reached across her to refill Leah's soup bowl. "You've had a terrible experience, Leah. Of course there are no such things as ghosts," the matronly Mrs. Hanson declared, "but that doesn't mean your fear wasn't real. I'd be plenty scared myself if I got locked in a closet by accident. What you need is a good hearty meal and a warm bath and lots of TLC."

Leah looked up into Mrs. Hanson's sparkly gray eyes. The pleasant-looking woman hardly resembled her sister, Alicia Preston, except around the eyes. She was round and short, where Madame was tall, still ballerina-thin, and very elegant. But tonight Leah had glimpsed another resemblance between the two sisters: Madame had her maternal side, too. Seeing that made Leah's ordeal in the closet almost worth it.

Leah dug into her second bowl of steamy chicken soup and basked a moment in the sense of being pampered. A pleasant drowsy feeling gradually took over her body, and the last shadowy fears that lingered in the corner of her mind seemed to vanish. Then Linda broke the spell.

"If you ask me," the strong-minded girl pronounced, "I think Pam had some nerve, treating you like her errand girl. It would have been more in character for her to ask Abigail!"

"Abby was late for class, too," Kay mused. She studied the paper napkin in front of her and absently doodled a cartoony picture of a fat ballerina with glasses and extremely bowed legs in a contorted arabesque.

"But Abby didn't know where Leah was, and Pam did. She should have told Madame. She would have saved everyone a lot of trouble," Linda insisted.

"Saving people trouble is not Pamela's style," Alex observed.

"True," Leah agreed. "But from what I heard, she told Madame I went to get her shoes. How was Pam supposed to know the closet door was going to slam shut behind me?"

"I wouldn't put it past Pamela Hunter to have sent you on an errand to get you in some kind of trouble. Maybe she didn't know about the door, but if she did, she sure wouldn't be in a rush to tell anyone," Linda insisted.

Suzanne strolled over to the refrigerator and poured herself some milk. She waved the carton in Leah's direction, but Leah was too stuffed to eat or drink anything more. When Suzanne returned to the table, her angular face was screwed up in a puzzled expression. "Do you really think Pam would get Leah in trouble with Madame just because of that *FootNotes* article?"

Kay, Alex, and Linda all nodded.

Leah cleared her throat. "But Pam didn't mean to get me in trouble. If I hadn't gotten stuck in the closet, I would have been only a minute or two later to rehearsal than Pam or Abby were."

"Abby—" Kay said suddenly. She banged her Magic Marker on the table, then quickly clapped her hand over her mouth. She beckoned the other girls closer and lowered her voice. "I think Alex hit the nail on the head."

"What did I say?"

"You said there's no wind in the basement." Kay leaned forward and checked to see that Mrs. Hanson was still out of the room. "I hate to say this, but I think that door did not close on you by accident."

Leah burst out laughing. "So we're back to the ghost theory!" It was easy to laugh now about poor Letitia Moorehouse. In the warm glow of the boardinghouse kitchen the whole idea of a ghost seemed ridiculous.

"I'm not talking about ghosts. I'm talking about the prime motive for anything that ever happens around this place." Kay paused for effect. She ruffled her fingers through her short black curls, then said solemnly, "Competition, of course."

"What are you getting at?" Linda demanded.

"I don't think Pam was the culprit this time. I agree with Leah on that. But don't any of you remember what happened to Abby today?"

"She felt sick during the grand entrance and ran out of the room," Alex said in a bored voice.

"Right. She left the room. Probably around the same time the door mysteriously slammed shut in Leah's face, locking her in the closet."

"Come off it," Linda cried. "Abby doesn't have the guts for something like that. She's a wimp."

"But—she's also Leah's understudy for both the mazurka and the pas de trois. If Leah gets in trouble with Madame or anyone else, it won't do Pam any good," Kay explained with a toss of her head. "But it sure would help Abby!"

Leah pushed her chair back from the table and stood up. "Listen, Kay, I think you're crazy. Abigail Handhardt is not my favorite person around here, and she's always been Pam's best friend, but I am sure she did not go running down to the basement in the middle of a rehearsal to lock me in a closet." Leah tightened the belt to her robe and looked at the clock. It was getting late, and she could barely keep her eyes open, let alone follow Kay's crazy train of thought. "How would she even know that's where Pam sent me to look for the boots? How would she know I was still down there?" Leah stretched her arms above her head and yawned. "It just doesn't make sense."

"Leah is right, and I also agree with Linda. Abby is too much of a wimp to lock Leah in a closet just to get Madame mad and steal Leah's roles," Alex commented.

"It was all just an accident!" Leah said with great firmness, wanting to end the discussion once and for all.

Chapter 9

"*Linda, how in the world did you get my mail?*" Leah snatched the bundle of envelopes from Linda's hand and tapped her foot against the linoleum floor of the dressing room, waiting for some kind of reasonable answer. She hoped Linda could think of one before Madame's class started. After last night's incident in the wardrobe room, Leah did not want to walk into morning class either late or upset. Finding two weeks worth of missing mail in Linda's dance bag certainly had the potential to make Leah more than upset.

"I have no idea." Linda looked as shocked as Leah. She peered into the depths of her new purple carryall and shook her head. "I don't get it."

"Oh, no!" Pamela wailed from over by the door that led to the Blue Studio. "Linda's bag is purple, too!"

"I know—I just know what's going to come next!" Kay muttered under her breath.

Pam either didn't hear Kay or pretended she

hadn't. She marched up to Leah, her green eyes bright with tears. "I'm sorry, Leah. I guess I got this all mixed up. I thought I was doing you a favor, and now I just made you mad." Pam's voice caught in her throat, and the frown on Leah's face turned to an expression of real concern.

She shook the redhead's shoulder gently. "Pam, what's wrong?"

"I knew how busy you've been, what with rehearsals and the way Robson's been rattling you, and I just wanted to save you some trouble, so when I've gone to pick up my mail, I've picked up yours, too," Pam explained.

Leah's chin jutted forward in dismay. "You've done *what*?" This was worse than eavesdropping on phone conversations: stealing mail was actually a federal offense. Leah bristled. But before she could say more, Pam quickly went on.

"Well, we do live in the same boardinghouse, and I always go down early for my mail—"

"*Before* Emily's there—" Alex pointed out a little sharply.

"Why, yes, the door to the post office is always open before class starts. And I must have accidentally put the mail in Linda's bag. I thought it was yours, Leah, really I did."

Leah didn't believe Pam, but she decided to take a closer look at Linda's new dance bag. Sure enough, it was the exact same color as Leah's, and it was made of the same soft kind of cloth. Leah had to admit that an honest mistake like that could have been made.

"But why didn't you ever tell me you were picking up my mail?" Leah asked Pam quietly. She quickly riffled through the letters: there were four from Chrissy and two from her mom, and a flyer from Hannah Greene's School of Dance and Theater Arts.

"I guess you'll never forgive me for this," Pam observed in a wounded voice.

"Spare me!" Linda grumbled. "And next time don't make it look like someone else did your dirty work, Pam." Without another word to Leah, Linda flounced out of the room, still cursing under her breath.

"What dirty work?" Pam snapped.

"Think about it, Pam. Leah's mail is missing, she gets locked in a closet, and it's all because of you," Kay said.

"No one's accusing you of anything, Pam," Leah said, staring pointedly at Kay. Kay gave a careless shrug that seemed to say, "I tried to warn you," and headed into the studio to begin her warm-up.

Alex lingered a moment longer, and from the look on her face, Leah could tell her Russian friend had something on her mind. Whatever she was going to say, Alex obviously thought better of it. She checked the mirror, gave a final pat to her tight neat topknot, and left the dressing room still pulling up her leg warmers.

Leah stood silent for a minute and tried to make sense of what had happened. Linda finding Leah's missing mail in her bag had shaken Leah more than she liked to admit, even to herself. Maybe it was the aftereffect of her harrowing experience of the night before, but Leah felt extra sensitive today, as if she had to be careful of something. The whole way to school she kept thinking how her life was beginning to feel booby-trapped. She was almost surprised that nothing terrible happened during the quarter mile walk from Mrs. Hanson's: no manhole covers were lying open in her path, no bottle fell out of the sky and bopped her on the head, no truck nearly ran her over. But just as she was beginning to feel safe and secure and that nothing weird was going to happen to her again, Linda discovered Leah's missing mail. She took a deep breath and walked over to the mirror. With a few deft strokes of her brush she swept her waist-length hair back from her face and up off her neck. She secured it quickly with an elastic and twisted her ponytail into a tidy bun.

Pam's voice frightened Leah. She had forgotten Pam was still in the dressing room. "Do you forgive me?" she asked timidly. The sweet little-girl tone didn't fit Pam at all. Leah looked quickly at Pam's reflection in the mirror and frowned.

"It was a mistake—I guess," Leah said tersely.

"I am sorry," Pam finally said.

"Okay, you're sorry." Leah whirled around, then softened her expression. Pam looked pale and a little shaken this morning, too. Leah figured she had stayed out late with her parents the night before.

Leah took a deep breath and forced herself to keep calm. "Pam, I'm sorry you misplaced my mail, too. It caused some problems for me. But just do me a a favor—"

"Anything, Leah. I owe you one—after that business in the closet and all."

Leah brushed off Pam's half-hearted apology; she didn't want to talk about the closet episode yet again. "That's over and done with. But Pam, next time you want to do me a favor, don't."

"It was an honest mistake!" Pam insisted.

"I never said it wasn't," Leah snapped. She grabbed her bag and hurried from the dressing room. She didn't trust herself to say more. She believed Pam, but she was afraid she'd start some kind of fight if she kept talking to her. The one thing Leah didn't need today was an argument before Madame's class. Leah had a sneaky suspicion that although Madame had been warm and understanding the night before, she'd be keeping a close eye on Leah. Leah knew she was treading a fine line where Madame was concerned, and she didn't want to make any more mistakes.

That night Leah got out of the royal blue SFBA van and waved good-bye to Katrina and Finola as Raul pulled away from the curb in front of Mrs. Hanson's. It was almost nine o'clock, and a fine rain was falling. Leah took a deep breath, turned the collar of her jacket up around her face, and shouldered her bag. She trudged up the short flight of steps leading to the boardinghouse porch, trying to remember when she'd last been so tired. Leah had spent ten hours of a twelve-hour day dancing, most of the time on pointe, and her feet were ready to fall off. She had performed poorly in Madame's class, stumbling over her own feet in the petite batterie, usually one of her strong points. And the day had ended on a sour note: three times she blanked out on the same passage of choreography in Odette's second act solo—though she had been studying the variation for over a year now, first with Miss Greene, and now under Andrei's tutelage. Andrei had made everything worse when he told Katrina that the way her understudies were dancing, it was a good thing she had won the role of the Swan Queen.

Leah stopped at the sign-in book and poked her head in the kitchen. She had skipped lunch but was too tired to bother with heating the stew Mrs. Hanson had left on the stove. She grabbed a cookie and poured herself a glass of milk. Leah leaned against the doorframe, munching her snack, too tired to think about anything seriously. On the way out of the kitchen, she noticed her kitten Misha's bowls were still full. "Funny," Leah commented to herself as she flicked out the kitchen light and headed for the stairs. Misha never left his food. The kitten had a fierce appetite and a clever way of conning every girl in the boardinghouse into feeding him. Leah grinned. Misha's untouched meal was probably his fifth of the night! It was the first time all day she had smiled. Thinking of Misha always made Leah happy. Halfway up the first flight of stairs Leah looked back over her shoulder. She sighed a soft, wistful sigh and cast a longing glance toward Pam's bedroom door. It was closed, and Misha was probably inside. She wished her own cat would sleep on her bed and not Pam's.

Upstairs Leah brushed her teeth, splashed water on her face, and in spite of her aching muscles decided to skip the bath she'd been looking forward to. A shower in the morning would just have to do. She could barely keep her eyes open long enough to get back to her room. She fell onto her bed with her bathrobe on and a tube of face cream in her hand. She just wanted to close her eyes for a few minutes, and then she'd get up and put the cream on her face, brush her hair, and take off her eye makeup.

The room was warm and the soothing patter of rain on the roof lulled Leah to sleep. At first she dreamed the dreams she always did on days when she'd been dancing too long and too hard, dreams where she was dancing the same steps again and again as if she were a wind-up doll unable to stop until she finally broke or wound down. The dream shifted to a vision of herself onstage. She wore a droopy blue tutu that sagged at the waist and with straps that kept sliding off her shoulders, hampering the movement of her arms. Midway through a variation she looked down and saw she was dancing on pointe wearing her mazurka boots and a moth-eaten pair of orange leg warmers. The audience was laughing, and she heard some-one shout up to the stage that he had paid forty bucks to see *Swan Lake*, not a half-baked skit from *Saturday Night Live*. Mortified, Leah fell off pointe and clomped her way across the stage in her boots, holding the bodice of her costume up with one hand.

In the wings she saw Madame, standing with her arms folded across her chest and a grim expression on her face. Leah reached out to hug her, to say she was sorry for not being the dancer Madame had wanted her to be, when Madame vanished. Leah ran farther into the wings and found herself running up a spiral staircase. Sud-denly the high walls on either side of Leah fell away, and Leah stopped, afraid to go farther, afraid to go back down, unable to move. Behind her she heard a voice calling her name. Leah forced her-self to look down, and far below she saw the figure of a woman rushing up the stairs toward her at incredible speed. The woman was slender and tall; long hair streamed out behind her as she ran. When she got closer, Leah realized she could see right through her. She looked up at her face and tried to scream, but no sound came out of her throat. It was Letitia Moorehouse: the face, the eyes, the incredibly sad smile on her full pouty lips. But the sepia-toned photo hadn't prepared Leah for the green glow of Letty's eyes or the red of her hair. As she watched Letitia's face shifting in and out of focus, it suddenly turned into someone else. Leah found her voice and cried out in horror, "It's Pam!"

Leah sat bolt upright in bed, her hand on her throat. "It was a dream!" Her relieved sigh filled the small room. "It was a dream!" This time she said it and smiled and fell back straight on her bed wondering why in the world she was sleeping in her bathrobe. She turned to her nightstand and gaped at the clock: it was 6:45, time for her to get up. Leah swung her feet out of bed. The attic room had grown cold in the night, and Leah sat on the edge of her bed and chafed her arms briskly. She wanted to make the cold go away. Most of all, she wanted to forget the terrible dream.

With heavy eyes she stood up and tried to stretch her stiff muscles. She shouldn't have skipped that bath last night, but a long hot shower now would help a little. For the first time since coming to SFBA in September, the prospect of another twelve-hour day of dancing daunted Leah. She slipped on her flip-flops and shuffled down the hall and into the bathroom. Abigail's door was still closed, but Leah could hear her hair dryer going and the sound of her favorite morning talk show on her radio. Usually Leah prided herself on being the first girl up and into the shower, but today she was glad Abby had beaten her. It wouldn't matter how long Leah luxuriated beneath the stream of hot water.

Leah turned on the water full blast and stepped

in. The steamy torrent soothed her back, and slowly Leah felt her neck and shoulders begin to relax. She reached for her shampoo, which was tucked in a niche in the tiled wall. With closed eyes she felt the various plastic containers, until her fingers closed around her bottle of shampoo. She picked it up and squeezed some into her hand. A strong odor filled the shower. It was a familiar smell like some kind of bathroom cleaning product. Absently, Leah wondered if Mrs. O'Callahan, who came in twice a week to help Mrs. Hanson clean, had come in early. Leah massaged the shampoo into her hair. She scrubbed and scrubbed, but the shampoo didn't lather as well as usual. She dumped more shampoo directly from the bottle onto her hair.

Leah suddenly recognized the sharp smell: it was ammonia. Leah frowned, then opened her eyes. Her hands were covered with some kind of awful brown stuff. Leah lifted her face to the water and rinsed the suds off her face; they were stinging her eyes. She opened her eyes again, and this time they burned only slightly. Leah looked at her hands again. They were still just as brown! So were her shoulders, her stomach, every place the water was running down from her head onto her body.

"*Ooooooooooo!!!!*" she cried, and jumped all at once out of the shower. She grabbed the nearest towel and scrubbed her skin. The color didn't come off. With the edge of the towel she cleared the mist off the mirror and let out a dreadful cry. "My hair!" Her blond hair was all matted down and had turned the strangest shade of brown. The color was running down the sides of Leah's face and neck in tiny dark rivulets, staining her skin.

"Alex!" Leah cried. She wrapped her towel around her and ran into the hallway. She didn't stop to turn off the water or close the bathroom door.

"Alex!" she shouted again, and bolted down the stairs. The door to Alex's room flew open, and Alex hurried into the hall.

"Your hair!!!!" Alex gasped when she saw Leah.

"What am I going to do?" Leah cried.

Chapter 10

Alex steered Leah right back up the stairs, where steam from the shower filled the narrow hall. The tall Russian girl closed the bathroom door behind them and turned off the shower. Then she sat Leah down on the edge of the tub.

"Hair color," she proclaimed. "The permanent kind. You washed your hair with permanent hair color." Alex met Leah's surprised blue eyes and started to smile. "I promise not to laugh," Alex said, sensing that Leah was not the least bit amused. She reached past Leah for the ribbed plastic bottle. It was half full of strong-smelling dark liquid. Alex held her nose with one hand and tossed the bottle in the trash. "I am sure you did not do this on purpose," she said.

"Of course I didn't. I reached for my shampoo. It was up there." Leah jumped up and yanked the fish-patterned shower curtain open and pointed to the niche. Only two plastic bottles were on the narrow shelf, and Leah's shampoo wasn't one of them. Leah stared in disbelief. "I don't get it," she said. "I keep my shampoo in the same sort of bottle. It's always there, right next to Abby's conditioner and my camomile stuff."

Alex whistled softly. "Leah, someone has played a very dirty trick on you. Someone put hair color in your shampoo bottle and wanted you to do this to yourself." Alex looked at Leah one minute longer, then grabbed a washcloth from a rack by the sink. She loaded it with soap and began to scrub Leah's shoulders and back. She rubbed Leah's skin so hard, it felt as if it were going to peel right off.

After a moment Alex waved the brown-stained cloth in front of Leah's face. "It does come off." She grabbed another clean washcloth from a shelf and handed it to Leah. "Get where you can reach. I will do your back."

"But my hair ..." Leah wailed, and hesitantly touched her head.

"That is not the big problem right now. When we get the color off the rest of you, shampoo your hair at least ten times. Most of it will come out. It will just be a little streaky, I think." Alex touched Leah's head and smiled encouragingly.

Leah didn't have the guts to look at herself in the mirror. She vigorously scrubbed the streaks of dye off her face and arms and chest. For a few minutes the girls worked in silence, concentrating on getting every last drop of brown dye off Leah. "So you really think someone did this on purpose," Leah finally said.

"Of course! How else does a mistake like this happen?" Alex regarded Leah with serious dark eyes. "I know you do not want to hear about Pam, but I think—"

"You think it was Pam." Leah nodded reluctantly. Her dreams lately had been about Pam, who was usually chasing or scaring her somehow. Leah didn't know much about dreams, but she trusted them. And maybe when she was asleep, Leah could see more clearly what she didn't want to look at when she was awake. Besides the dreams, there were the crazy incidents of the locked closet and the lost mail. Evidence was beginning to point to Pam. It seemed Leah's friends had been right—Pamela Hunter was still out to get her.

"Of course, Pam doesn't dye her hair this color." Alex sounded thoughtful, as if she were mulling something over. "Maybe it is Pam—or maybe Kay is right."

"What did Kay say?" So much had happened over the last few days, Leah couldn't even remember when she last really talked to Kay.

"That Abigail had more of a motive to scare you than Pam. She does understudy both your parts. Whether you dance or not, Pam gets to go on."

"Abby?" Leah shook her head. "Abby wouldn't do something like this. She's not—" Leah fished for the word. She pictured Abigail, slight, quiet, with mousy brown hair ... "Abby's hair!" Leah cried, then lowered her voice. "She dyed it. I forgot all about that!"

Alex propped herself against the sink and looked up at the ceiling. "Are we dumb, or are we dumb? And she dyed it dark brown. I think the color in the bottle was dark brown."

"So she might have left it there by accident, in the shower!" Leah felt relieved. No one was playing tricks on her, it was all just an accident.

"Wrong!"

"Why?"

"Because that was over a week ago. Leah Stephenson, you have washed your hair other times this week, no?"

Leah nodded. She washed it almost every day. She finished Alex's thought for her. "And this didn't happen until now." Leah washed out the facecloth and braved a look in the mirror. Her face was clean, but her hair looked terrible. "Ugh!" she grimaced. She allowed herself one more moment of pure despair, then squared her shoulders and turned back to Alex.

"I have no idea what Abby—or Pam, or anyone else for that matter—would gain by doing this."

"Someone wants to rattle you, to make you nervous," Alex pointed out. "To cause you to mess up enough that you'll get into trouble. You're a good dancer, Leah—more than a good dancer. Jealousy makes people do strange things."

The breakfast bell rang, and Leah stopped Alex from continuing with her theory. "You go downstairs. There's no point in both of us getting in trouble today. I'll start washing my hair. Just tell Mrs. Hanson I overslept. Make up something. Please don't tell her the truth," Leah pleaded.

Alex looked reluctant, but she agreed. "Put a scarf on your hair. Madame won't like it, but you can tell her you tried to bleach it. She'll be angry, but she'll understand it was an accident. Just make sure you are not late to class today." She probably sensed that Madame was already annoyed with Leah. Alex had an uncanny sense of the director's moods. Leah couldn't worry about being late now. She'd clean up as fast as she could. Seven times she washed her hair, then she held a strand up in front of her eyes. It still looked darker than normal and oddly streaked, but most of the hair color was gone.

Ten minutes later Leah was dressed and tying a deep purple scarf around her topknot. Her blond hair looked splotchy green in places, but Leah could live with that. If she got a chance, she'd go to the local salon before Thursday and get the color evened out before the big performance. She bounced down the stairs, trailing her coat and dance bag behind her. The dining room was already deserted, and Leah could hear Mrs. Hanson vacuuming her own bedroom. Leah ducked into the kitchen and grabbed a banana from the fruit bowl on the Formica counter. She glanced at the clock. If she ran the whole way to school, she still had a chance of making it to class on time.

As Leah headed out the kitchen door, she glanced down at Misha's bowls. The milk looked as if it had curdled, and it filled the bowl to the brim—just like the night before. The cat food was still heaped high, and Leah could have sworn Misha hadn't touched it.

"Misha!" Leah called.

She waited a moment, then wandered into the hall. The door to Pam's room was open. Pam's bed was still unmade. From where she stood, Leah could see Misha wasn't in his usual spot, curled up on the rumpled down quilt. "Misha!" she called again, a little louder. Then she whistled; that never failed to get him. When he didn't come, Leah shifted nervously from foot to foot, then bent down and started looking under the furniture in the living room. She checked the windowsill, Suzanne's sewing basket, and the magazine rack near the stereo, but the red kitten was nowhere to be found.

Maybe he's sick, Leah thought. Just then the cuckoo clock started chiming—it was already nine o'clock.

"Oh, no!" Leah wailed. "I'm really late now." She wavered only a minute in the front hall. All her instincts prompted her to look for her kitten—if he was sick or hurt, he might need help fast. On the other hand, if she skipped morning class ... Leah shuddered at what the consequences might be. She was already in hot water with Madame, and the scarf on her head was going to make things even worse. Leah grabbed a pencil and tore a sheet of paper out of the back of the sign-in book. She scribbled a quick note to Mrs. Hanson. "Misha is either sick or missing. If you get a chance, please look for him. Thanks. Leah."

Leah pinned the note to the message board and ran out the door. She dashed as fast as she could to school, cutting through a couple of backyards and the Academy's parking lot. As she pushed open the side door, she glanced at the face of the grandfather clock and grimaced. It was ten minutes after nine.

She bolted down the hall, past the auditorium. The smell of fresh paint hung in the air, and the carpenters' hammers still echoed through the corridor. Leah didn't bother to head down to her locker to hang up her coat or to check the notice board near the front staircase. She took the stairs two at a time and arrived in the dressing room of the Red Studio, breathless. It wasn't until she had her sweater off that she realized no sounds at all were coming from the studio itself. She frowned and wondered if Madame had just stopped class to yell at someone. Leah looked around the changing area and didn't quite believe her eyes: there were discarded toe shoes, one purple leg warmer, and a couple of sweaters thrown over the backs of chairs. It was the usual assortment of dressing room stuff, but no jackets or dance bags or other clothes were in sight. Leah threw open the door that led to the studio. It was empty.

Leah grabbed her stuff, dressed in her jeans and shoes and leotard, and hurried into the hall. The whole second floor was abnormally quiet. The only music she could hear was the faint beat of a rock song coming from the workmen's radio down in the auditorium. She squirmed back into her sweater and ran down the front stairs, almost stumbling as she reached the bottom. Desperately Leah tried to fight the feeling of panic in her chest. Where was everybody? It was now almost twenty-five minutes after nine. She had missed the warm-up, the beginning of class, and she had no idea where Madame Preston was teaching this morning. Leah headed for the auditorium. Maybe Madame had decided to use the stage. Leah knew that made no sense, but she walked in anyway. One of the painters greeted her with a questioning smile.

"Uh—do you know where everyone is?" Leah asked.

"No, not really," the bearded man said. "All I know is the school van came for a couple of loads of kids about half an hour ago."

Another painter spoke up from the stage. "Seems to me I heard something about a car pool."

"A car pool?" Leah closed her eyes and sank back against the doorframe. Obviously the class location had been changed, and no one had bothered to tell Leah. She hurried over to the bulletin board and found the notice right away. It was dated this morning. Leah scanned the message quickly: it confirmed an announcement made at afternoon corps rehearsal the day before. There would be a short morning class today, followed by full dress rehearsal on the Opera House stage, since the auditorium was still under construction. Leah hadn't been at yesterday's corps rehearsal. She had been rehearsing with Robson, and then had been called downstairs for a final costume fitting. But Pam had been at the corps rehearsal, and so had Abby, and Suzanne, and Kay, and Linda—everyone who lived at Mrs. Hanson's. But no one had told Leah. Her eyes stung with tears, but Leah forced herself to hold them back. Crying now wouldn't help a thing. She had to get to the Opera House before it was too late. She had no idea how she was going to explain this latest lapse of discipline to Madame, but if she missed the dress rehearsal, she'd be out of Thursday's performance for sure.

Leah hurried out the front door and made it to the bus stop just in time to see the downtown bus drive away. She threw her bag down on the sidewalk and wondered why her entire future as a dancer seemed to be jinxed lately. Leah heard the rumble of thunder, and a cold, heavy rain began to pour.

Chapter 11

"*Where have you been?*" *Katrina*
Gray cried, rushing up to Leah. In the murky
backstage light of the Opera House Katrina looked
radiant. She had on her snow-white tutu and one
of her mother's earth-toned hand-woven shawls
over her slim shoulders. Her large brown eyes
took in Leah's soggy purple scarf, the strands of
wet hair that had worked loose from her bun, and
the muddy spots on her tights where they showed
beneath her rolled-up jeans.

"I didn't know," Leah began, trying to catch her
breath. The bus had been caught in traffic, and
she had gotten off and run the last few blocks.
"No one told me about the class change. I was
late this morning," Leah had trouble getting the
words out. Everyone had known about the sched-
ule change; one look at the stage confirmed it.
Alex was onstage dressed like a lady of the court.
Kay was in the peasant corps and stood in a
corner pretending to chat with her partner. It was
the middle of the first act. Leah dropped her
dance bag with a thud and slipped out of her

soggy coat. The wool was soaking wet, and the coat smelled like a dog badly in need of a bath.

Leah stepped closer to the stage. Kevin Thompson, a senior, was dancing the role of Prince Siegfried. He was standing only a few feet from Leah, smiling in the direction of the opposite wing. Then familiar music started, and Abigail, Kenny, and Pam ran liltingly onto the stage. It was time for the pas de trois—*Leah*'s pas de trois—to begin. She caught her breath. "Abby's dancing my part!" she croaked in a loud whisper.

Katrina grabbed her arm. "Don't worry. You can explain to Madame. Something must have happened. You look terrible." Leah had no way to respond to Katrina. She was too busy staring at Abby. Kay's suspicions had been right on the mark. To get Leah's roles, Abby had somehow plotted not only to unnerve Leah but to be sure she missed the first dress rehearsal, a real sin in Madame's eyes and something sure to lose Leah the chance to dance at the scholarship performance Thursday night.

Pam and Kenny ran off into the opposite wing and Abby performed Leah's first short solo. Her interpretation made Leah cringe, as she spun in a series of jerky chaînés and pirouettes toward the wing next to Leah. Leah braced herself to confront her new enemy. Abby posed on one foot, then did a little ballet run offstage. A moment later she poked her head around to Leah's wing, and she struggled to catch her breath. "That's a dirty trick, Leah, not showing up today," she whined. "I'm not ready for this." Abby stamped her foot and shrugged off the towel Mia offered her. She looked at the stage; the cue for her next entrance was several minutes away.

Leah treated Abby to a cold stare, but when she did, she wondered if she had jumped to the wrong conclusion. Abigail Handhardt did not look like a girl who had triumphed and stolen a coveted part. In fact, she looked a little silly: she was wearing Leah's tutu, which drooped too low on her legs and was too tight across the bust. The straps were loose and slipped down onto her shoulders even as she talked. Leah wondered how she had ever managed to dance in it. Mrs. Slavinska would have to alter it fast if Abby went on to perform on Thursday evening. Abby looked worried, angry, and very tense. All at once Leah knew for sure Abby hadn't played all those tricks on her. She didn't have the guts to play games like that, and Leah could see that Abby wasn't ruthless enough, either. Abby would not kill to get a role—certainly not one she was barely prepared for.

Instinctively Leah's eyes sought Pam. Kenny was in the middle of his solo, and Pam had exited to the wing across from Leah. At first Leah couldn't quite get a glimpse of the redhead. Kenny was whirling high above the stage in a series of jetés en tournant and tours en l'air. His performance was brilliant, and in spite of her current predicament, Leah felt a thrill watching him. After he jetéd past Leah, she had a clear view of Pam. Pam stood opposite her, grinding the toes of her shoes in the rosin box. Then she carefully patted her hair in place. Soon she would begin her own bravura solo, the one with all the leaps that showed off her technique. The heavy stage makeup suited Pam's strong bone structure, and the rusty color of her costume complemented her auburn hair. She looked incredibly beautiful—and suspiciously self-satisfied. Pam finally peered across the stage, shielding her eyes from the spotlights. When she spotted Leah, the surprised look on her face gave her away. Pam obviously had not expected to see Leah Stephenson at this dress rehearsal. Leah was certain that Pam was the one who made her late today. Pam never intended that Leah would even show up at the Opera House.

Leah's impulse was to run across the stage and drag Pam out to stage center and accuse her right there and then in front of Madame Preston. But accuse her of what? Leah couldn't quite picture herself telling the world that Pam was trying to ruin her nerves. The effects of Pam's little campaign against her had been pretty devastating, but still Pam hadn't done anything wrong—at least nothing Leah could prove to Madame. Everything that had happened so far could look like an accident, even Leah's being late today. Because of Pam she had missed two rehearsals so far this week. So missing today's class would almost seem in character with a new, undisciplined, stuck-up Leah—the girl featured in the *FootNotes* article whose taste of fame went to her head.

Leah clenched her fists and stood her ground. She'd wait until Pam's variation was finished. Leah was pretty sure Pam would land in the same wing where she was standing.

"Leah, you finally got here." Alex came up behind Leah. She sounded so worried that Leah knew she was in big trouble. Behind her Suzanne gaped at Leah's soggy scarf and wet hair.

"I had no idea the dress rehearsal had been changed to today," Leah said simply, not accusing anyone. But she was still very hurt that Alex hadn't told her.

Alex stared at her. "I do not understand." Then Alex slapped her forehead with her hand. "Oh, Leah! Pam did not tell you. And this morning, with all the commotion over your hair I did not think—"

"What *did* happen to your hair?" Abby interrupted. She stared rudely at the brown-streaked strands lying damp and limp around Leah's face.

Feeling self-conscious, Leah tried to tuck her hair back into her bun, but it was useless. She tore off the soggy scarf, revealing her streaked, green-brown hair. What was the point of trying to hide it? Her hair was the least of her problems now.

"I didn't know class was *here*, either," Leah said.

"I am sorry, Leah. But Madame told Pam to tell you, and then—"

"Pam—yes, of course, Pam was supposed to tell me," Leah said in a defeated voice.

Pam's music started, and everyone quieted down to watch her variation. Leah took some small satisfaction when the redhead nearly missed her cue. *Look who's rattled now!* Leah gloated for a moment. But Pam quickly regained her composure and leapt onto the stage. Someone in the small audience of teachers, students, and company members gasped with amazement. No, Leah realized, Pam was too determined to ever let anything interfere with her dancing.

Leah now prepared herself to confront Pam. The flashy solo concluded with a series of split jetés on a diagonal across the stage, ending right in Leah's wing. Pam soared through the air, somehow controlling her elevation so each jump was higher than the last. With a grunt audible from the wings, Pam soared into her last jeté and landed right at Leah's feet. Leah should have reached out and steadied her, but she didn't.

Pam stumbled and stubbed her toe, but she looked right up at Leah after catching her balance. "You finally made it." She was panting after the exertion of her athletic variation, but her voice was as sweet as could be. "I was so worried about you, Leah. I thought something had happened. You didn't turn up for class. Alex told me something had happened back at the boardinghouse, but she said you'd be here. Madame kept wondering what was keeping you."

"She should have asked *you*, not Alex," Leah said. Leah couldn't believe how calm and steady she sounded—inside she was trembling with anger.

"What in the world do you mean by that?" Pam asked innocently.

"You were supposed to tell Leah yesterday about morning class, about how the dress rehearsal would be held here today. Madame told you to tell her. I heard her myself," Kay said, walking up. She offered her back to Alex to help her out of her peasant costume. Like most of the girls, Kay was in the corps in the ballet's first, second, and fourth acts. Quick changes were part of the rehearsal, too.

"I know I was," Pam admitted readily. She frowned and flicked a sequin off her arm. "But I never saw Leah—not last night, not this morning. It's not like I didn't tell her on purpose." There was a defensive note in Pam's voice, as if she were hinting that anyone could make a simple mistake. During the competition for the Louise Adams Scholarship, Leah had accidentally forgotten to tell Katrina about a change in practice schedules. Her oversight nearly lost Katrina her chance of winning—and staying at the school.

"That's not fair, Pam," Leah cried in a low, angry voice. She was very conscious of Katrina standing somewhere behind her, warming up her feet with a series of battements tendu.

"Nothing's fair or unfair," Pam retorted. She paused and added breezily, "Besides, what happened to the rest of your friends? They all knew about it." She grinned slyly at Alex. Then she looked back at Leah and softened her glance. "I mean, you of all people should know someone can make a dumb mistake and forget to pass on last-minute rehearsal information."

Kay immediately leapt to Leah's defense. "That's old news, Pamela Hunter."

Pam didn't reply. She looked at the stage and poked Abby in the ribs. "You missed your cue!"

From down in the orchestra pit Robert's piano stopped. Christopher Robson stormed onto the stage and glared into the wings. Abigail shrunk back in dismay. "Sorry, Mr. Robson—I got confused." Her next words made Leah want to strangle her. "I didn't know if I should finish—or if Leah should go on."

The scowl on Robson's face vanished. "Leah?" He shaded his eyes from the lights and headed toward the wing. The worried look on his face startled Leah. "Here at last!" He looked her up and down, taking in her wet clothes, stringy hair, and the fact she wasn't dressed for class, let alone rehearsal. "Madame said you were to see her as soon as you arrived." His voice hardened as he glared at the other girls and said, "Didn't anyone tell her that?"

Even Alex looked away, embarrassed.

Leah pushed her damp hair off her face and straightened her shoulders. "Where is she?"

"She'll be in the dressing room at the top of the stairs. The one Diana uses during the season."

The other girls wandered away to change costume, and as soon as they were gone, Christopher put a hand on Leah's shoulder. "You've worked hard for this performance. Madame knows that. I told her this morning. Whatever made you miss class and rehearsal had to be important. You, not Abby, must dance on Thursday."

Leah was too upset to take in Christopher's words, but there was a kindness in his voice that surprised her. For a moment she just stared at him, trying to figure him out. The Christopher Robson she'd been rehearsing with for the past couple of weeks was not a kind man. Of course, being kind wasn't really part of his job. Leah suddenly realized all his criticism was to make every student dance his or her best. Leah's spirits lifted slightly. "Thank you" was all she managed to say, but she meant it.

Leah stopped to gather her things and, with the sleeve of her coat trailing behind her, crossed the stage behind the backdrop and headed up the narrow metal steps to the hall. Even before she left the backstage area the music had begun again, and Abby was back under the lights, performing Leah's last solo.

Leah paused outside Diana's dressing room door, then knocked softly and walked in.

Madame was sitting on the stool in front of Diana's dressing table, and Leah stood awkwardly in front of her. Alicia Preston's eyes widened slightly as she looked at Leah. Otherwise, her stern face betrayed no emotion.

"Sit down, Leah," Madame said very quietly.

Leah looked around. There were two other chairs in the room, both heaped with Diana's clothes. Gingerly she pushed aside a pile of tights and sat down on the edge of the chair. She put her coat and bag down at her feet.

"I am very disappointed in you, Leah," Madame began.

Leah's brow creased in a frown. "I'm sorry—"

With a sharp gesture Madame raised her hand for Leah to be quiet. "Sorry is not a word I like to hear. Not when one of the most gifted students I have ever seen starts falling apart at the seams."

Madame's accusation stung, and Leah felt she had to defend herself. "I'm not falling apart—"

Alicia Preston's gray eyes narrowed. Leah knew the Academy director was not used to being contradicted, but at the moment Leah just didn't care.

"Madame." Leah tried to soften her tone, but her voice came out sounding shrill. "I couldn't help missing class today."

"Or rehearsal Saturday, or Sunday? Leah, look at yourself!" Madame stared pointedly at Leah's damp, muddied jeans and her stringy hair.

Leah didn't have to look. She lowered her head and clasped her hands together. When she spoke again, her voice pleaded for Madame to understand. "It wasn't my fault. None of it's been my fault, Madame. Something's been going on."

A frown flickered on Madame's face, but she motioned for Leah to continue.

"I certainly didn't lock myself in a closet. And I can't help it that no one told me about today's rehearsal change. I didn't lose my own mail—"

"What happened to your mail?" Madame asked.

Leah kept her mouth shut and studied her hands. The other night Madame had warned her about blaming other people—namely Pamela Hunter— for all her troubles. Leah wasn't going to blame Pam again—not until she could prove without a doubt that the competitive redhead was behind all the unsettling events of the past few weeks.

When Leah didn't respond to her question, Madame asked in a very gentle voice, "Leah, is something wrong? Are you having a problem I should know about?"

Leah was torn for a moment. Telling Madame now might just win the director's sympathy. On the other hand, accusing Pam without proof could cause Leah—and possibly Pam—trouble neither of them deserved.

"Nothing I can't handle myself," Leah said unsteadily.

"I'm afraid that's not true." Madame stood up and walked over toward the metal clothes rack. She absently fingered Diana's costumes. "Whatever is going on, a dancer—a real dancer—cannot buckle under the pressure. If you think there is pressure in this school, wait until you move up into a company. The competition is fierce. You can never afford to perform at less than your best." She paused, then went on more slowly. "I am not talking about your dancing itself. Some days a dancer is stronger than others. But I am talking about your sense of discipline, of being able to rise above whatever catastrophes occur around you." She walked slowly to the dressing table and leaned against it. She looked directly at Leah as she spoke. "I had the hope when you first came here that you were made of tougher stuff than you seem to be. I thought you could weather the pressure—now I'm not sure. I am afraid that article in *FootNotes* has affected you badly, Leah. The San Francisco Ballet Academy will not tolerate temperamental prima donnas on its premises—not as long as I'm the director."

"That's not fair, Madame," Leah said, the anger spilling out of her in a torrent. She jumped up and looked right at Madame Preston. "You have no reason to accuse me of being temperamental. Sure, I've had a crazy week, and I haven't been at my best. I'm not looking to be excused for what happened—even if it wasn't my fault. But everyone's entitled to goof up now and then. *Everyone.*"

"Not a real ballerina!" Madame said with great force. "Never a real ballerina. Imagine Margot Fonteyn missing class and coming to rehearsal looking like—that!" Madame waved a hand in Leah's face.

Leah kicked at the floor with the toe of her soggy sneaker. "Well, I guess I'm not Fonteyn, then."

"No, I guess you're not." The sadness and disappointment in Madame's voice was almost too much to bear. Leah felt as if she was going to cry.

For a moment neither of them said anything. Then Leah spoke up, her blue eyes brimming with tears. "So I guess I should forget about—" Leah wanted to say forget about school, about ever dancing again, about trying to be a ballerina, but Madame didn't give her the chance.

"Forget about today, and prove to me tomorrow that you are worthy of dancing on Thursday. Then you can have your part back."

Chapter 12

"*Misha's not here?*" Leah clutched the open door of the boardinghouse and searched the faces in front of her for some ray of hope.

"Come in out of the rain, Leah," Mrs. Hanson put her arm around Leah's shoulder and drew her into the house. "You'll catch a cold, dear, and that won't help solve a thing, now, will it?" She tried to guide Leah to the kitchen, where she was baking something that smelled delicious, but Leah refused to budge.

"I don't believe this!" Now she looked around: Alex, Kay, Suzanne, Abby, and Linda were all there, but Pam was not. The vague terrible thought Leah had had on her way back from the Opera House finally took shape. "Pam stole my cat. I know she did. She has Misha!" The tears Leah hadn't shed in front of Madame, or when she walked in late to rehearsal, or when she discovered the Red Studio deserted this morning, suddenly poured right out of her. She buried her face in her hands and slumped against the wall, sobbing uncontrollably.

"Pam stole Misha?" Alex sounded so incredulous, Leah had to look up.

"That's a pretty wild accusation," Mrs. Hanson said quietly, coming to Leah's side. She put her fingers under Leah's chin and gently raised her face to look in her eyes.

Leah pursed her lips and blinked away her tears. She had no time to explain to Mrs. Hanson now. She had to find Misha. Later she would tell everyone what Pam had done to her.

Mrs. Hanson looked around the circle of girls and seemed to realize that everyone would speak more openly if she left. "If you girls need me, or anyone wants to talk to me, I'll be in the back parlor," she offered.

No one said a word until the door to the back half of the house, Mrs. Hanson's own private suite of rooms, closed behind her.

Alex took Leah's hand and led her into the living room. "We will find Misha. We will talk for a minute or two, then we will look. Misha is fine, Leah. I feel that." Alex paused. When she continued to speak, a wry smile played around her full lips. "I am Russian, remember, with tea-leaf-reading grandparents. I see the future. I do not feel that Misha is in grave danger."

Leah suspected that Alex was laughing at her; but at the same time she wanted to trust Alex's instincts. Leah took a deep breath, then plunged into her latest theory about Pam. She began with her interview with Madame, leaving out only the final comment about Fonteyn. That was a deep hurt Leah would never share with anyone. When she finished, the other girls looked horrified.

"At least Madame told you to try again tomorrow, Leah," Abby said.

Leah knew Abby was trying to be helpful, but she didn't feel like thanking her for her support, not now. "I took the bus home. Rehearsal was almost over. I was upset, I guess." As she talked, Leah shrugged off her wet sweater and began to pull the hairpins from the shambles of her bun. "I got on the wrong bus and ended up down by the airport. It was a long ride back, and I had plenty of time to think." She looked at Abby and hesitated, then decided she didn't care who was or wasn't supposed to be Pam's best friend. "I realized Pam was behind everything—"

"You mean the mouse and all that?" Abby asked, shocked.

"Yes, Abby," Alex commented. "She and Leah have had their problems. You know that. Pamela does not like Leah at all. She has tried to hurt her before," Alex reminded Abby. "But, Leah, I do not see what Misha has to do with this."

"She's been trying to get at me, to rattle me. What better way than to steal my cat!"

"Steal your cat?" Pam had just walked in the door. She was wearing her good coat and high shiny boots. She looked fabulous, as if she were dressed for a very important date. But Leah could not believe the worried expression on Pam's face.

Pam tossed her purse on a chair and marched up to Leah. "Who stole Misha?"

"Come off it, Hunter!" Leah cried, scrambling to her feet. She shoved her green-streaked hair out of her face and glared at the other girl. "My cat's been missing since Sunday night, and you know where he is. This is pretty mean, Pam. This is worse than the mouse in my shoe, worse than locking me in a closet, worse than anything I ever

imagined you capable of doing. If Misha is—"
Leah clapped her hands to her mouth. She was
afraid to voice her worst fear.

"I would never, ever, hurt that cat!" Pam cried.
Beneath her perfect makeup her face had gone
white. "I love him!"

"Don't make me sick, Hunter!" Leah spat. She
walked right up to Pam, and with her face only
inches from hers, Leah spelled out her threat.
"Ever since that *FootNotes* article, you've been
out to get me. Even before that. My mail disap-
pearing was no accident." Pam took a step backward and looked at the other girls, her eyes large
with fear. "As soon as I find that cat I am going to
Madame and tell her everything, Pam."

"Calm down, Leah," Alex whispered. "If Pam
has Misha, you are only going to make things
worse."

"I don't believe you," Pam sputtered. She ran
off to her room and slammed the door.

Alex turned to the other girls. "We will orga-
nize a search party. Linda, Kay—check the basement. I remember he goes down there sometimes
when the door is open." She took charge and
assigned the other girls specific areas of the house.
Just as they headed out of the living room, Pam's
door burst open.

"I found him. I found him!" Her cry was triumphant.

Leah whirled around. The expression of pure
joy on Pam's face checked her next words, at
least for the moment. Was Pamela Hunter that
good an actress? The redhead was clutching the
kitten, who was blissfully licking her cheek.

Leah watched for only a second. "Give me my

cat!" She grabbed Misha, who gave a startled mew and squirmed away. He jumped to the floor, stretched, then headed straight for his bowls.

"Where was he?" several girls asked at once.

"In my hamper," Pam said, still looking at Leah. Her bottom lip was trembling and her green eyes were shining with tears. "In my wicker hamper. I left it open on Sunday when I did my laundry, and when I closed it, he must have been inside. I haven't been around or I would have noticed sooner—Leah, stop looking at me like that!" Pam cried suddenly.

"I don't believe you. I didn't think even you would sink this low. I'm not waiting until tomorrow. I'm phoning Madame right now. Who knows what or who you'll try to hurt next!"

Pam stepped in front of Leah, blocking the way to the hall telephone. "Okay," she cried shrilly. "Call Madame, I don't care. If I get kicked out of here, I don't care about that either. Yes, Leah," Pam sneered. "I hid your mail on purpose in Linda's bag—"

"You creep!" Linda cried, her dark eyes flashing.

Pam went on without missing a beat. "Misha brought me a mouse one night and I figured the Great Stephenson could use a surprise or two to make her life a tad more interesting." The hatred in Pam's voice shocked Leah. She pressed her back against the doorway, wishing Pam would just stop. Leah wasn't sure she could bear to hear anymore.

"I locked you in the closet!"

Kay gasped. "She could have died down there."

"Oh, Larkin, stop being melodramatic. No one ever died from a few hours in a closet and a couple of skipped meals." Pam turned her wrath once again on Leah. "I even had you convinced about Letitia's ghost." Pam let out an arch little laugh. "Really, Leah, you are such a farm girl."

Leah bristled, but before she could defend herself Pam went on. "I did it. I did everything you accused me of. But I did *not* hide or hurt Misha. Nothing in the world would make me do a thing like that. What kind of girl do you think I am anyway?"

Leah gaped at Pam. "I don't know, Pam. But from what you just confessed to, I'd say the kind of girl I wish I had never met!" Leah pushed past Pam but didn't stop at the phone. She started up the stairs. Something about Pam's confession bothered Leah. She didn't feel so strongly about going to Madame anymore. Going to the head of the school meant two things: Leah would be the cause of Pam being kicked out, and Pam would probably never have a career in dance. Leah shuddered at the thought. Ratting on someone, on anyone, was something Leah had never done, not once in her whole life. Starting now felt wrong. It felt like something someone else would do—someone like Pam.

The next morning Leah was the first girl down for breakfast. It was half past seven when Leah padded down the stairs, and the smell of fresh brewed coffee drifted up from the kitchen. She reached the bottom and turned the corner to head for the dining room. From the living room she heard the sound of voices, angry voices that at first she didn't recognize. Then she realized one of the voices belonged to Pam. Leah stood frozen to the spot, not quite sure what to do. Against her better judgment Leah crept back down the hall and pressed herself flat against the wall. She knew she shouldn't listen, but who would Pam be arguing with at this hour? Leah's curiosity got the best of her.

"Mother, you don't understand a thing!" Pam cried, the pain in her voice evident. Leah had completely forgotten that Pam's parents were in town for the performance.

"I understand only one thing, Pamela, and that is that you have been a very great disappointment to me and your father." Leah cringed at the very sound of Mrs. Hunter's voice. She spoke with a deeper drawl than her daughter. She sounded cultured and sophisticated, and very, very cold.

"Disappointment?" Pamela sneered and Leah could just picture the look of contempt on her face. "Why, Mommy dearest, I only got into the top ballet school in the country—"

"Where you are obviously not the top student at all! I cannot believe, Pamela Belle, that you let some little wimp of a girl steal the part of Odette/Odile out from right under your nose."

"Listen, I never told you I got the lead! I never said that!" Pam said, sounding very defensive.

"But what else could we think? You wrote and said you were dancing in *Swan Lake*. Miss Charlotte herself said you were a born Odile." Mrs. Hunter's voice took on a proud but dreamy tone, and Leah understood Pam's problems instantly. She had one of those mothers who wanted to be a ballet star herself and who pushed and pushed her daughter so hard to make her own dreams come true.

Leah closed her eyes and shook her head rue-fully. She had never suspected Pam came from a family like that. Hannah Greene's School of Dance and Theater Arts back in San Lorenzo was small, but Leah had seen her share of fanatic ballet moms. They were easy to spot: They pushed their daughters to be stars from day one. Their daughters were supposed to get the lead in the baby productions; they were supposed to win the prizes and go on and become the really big stars. Leah had often wondered if the daughters of women like that ever got very far at all. Leah's old rival at Miss Greene's school, Annie MacPhearson, had a mother like that. Annie was now an apprentice with the New York City Ballet, and her mom had given up her business and what was left of her marriage just to move to New York so Annie wouldn't have to face life in the big city alone. There had been another girl, whose name Leah couldn't remember but whose thin, pinched face she'd never forget. She had had a breakdown when she was only thirteen, and rumor had it she had become very fat. Now Leah understood why Andrei pitied Pam: he must have recognized the symptoms. Leah supposed they had ballet mothers in Russia, too.

Mrs. Hunter's voice rose and she said in a particularly nasty tone, "Who cares about a silly little first act pas de trois? We never would have come to see you dance if we had known you had been offered such a small role. It's an insult, Pamela Belle, and don't you forget it." Mrs. Hunter paused, and Leah couldn't catch Pam's next words. "But my dear," Mrs. Hunter said in a bored voice, "why would we stay to see you dance that? Your father and I are taking the ten o'clock flight home this morning."

"I don't believe this!" Pam practically screamed. "Why are you always trying to punish me?"

"Goodness, what dramatics!" Mrs. Hunter let out a bell-like laugh. "Pamela dearest, we are not trying to punish you. It seems you are your own worst enemy in the long run."

"Don't start in on that again!" Pam cried sharply.

"But you never learn from your mistakes, Pamela Belle. Never. You need to learn to push harder. I don't think you try hard enough. You've got to get yourself noticed more. You've got looks, talent, everything. When you didn't win that Golden Gate Award here, your father and I couldn't believe it."

"Mother—"

"I am not finished, Pamela Belle." Mrs. Hunter heaved a loud sigh, and Leah shook her head. Why was Pam's mother being so hard on her? Her attitude seemed downright cruel to Leah. Instantly Leah found herself comparing Pam's mom to Mr. Robson. Christopher was hard on his dancers, but he didn't knock them when they were down. She had seen that very clearly yesterday. He had been cruel to Pam, too, at moments—but he had also spurred her on to dance her best.

Mrs. Hunter went on. "Now it turns out you didn't even get a chance to understudy the lead after losing the Adams competition. Sometimes I think you don't even want to be a successful dancer."

"Maybe I don't!" Pamela snapped, and once again Leah recalled Andrei's comment about Pam dancing as if she hated it.

Mrs. Hunter dismissed Pam's comments quickly. "Don't be ridiculous! I think you were born to be a great ballerina."

"I think you're nuts," Pamela growled. "You're the one who wishes she were a great ballerina," Pam said with a sob in her voice. "I sometimes wish something would happen to me so I'd never dance again. That—that would serve you right."

In the hallway Leah stifled a gasp of horror. After a long pause Mrs. Hunter responded, "Don't you ever say anything like that again. After all we've done for you, the sacrifices we've made to give you the best dance education available!"

"Just so you'll look good, Mother, just so you'll look good."

"That's not true, Pamela." There was a hint of real affection in Mrs. Hunter's voice as she said, "I only want the best for you." Mrs. Hunter waited, as if to give Pam time to say something. "I'm not the only one who thinks you have exceptional talent: Miss Charlotte does, and so does Madame Preston. She told me that when I called to check on your progress."

"You called to *what*?"

Leah could empathize with Pam's shocked tone.

"To see how you were doing. She said you had a brilliant future in dance."

"She said that?" Pam sounded skeptical but pleased.

Leah felt a rush of jealousy. She wanted to be Madame's favorite student, not Pam.

"Yes. And she said that you worked hard and you only needed to become more sensitive and subtle—whatever that means." Mrs. Hunter's voice betrayed her feelings all too clearly. Being subtle was something Pam's mother definitely did not understand. Leah knew exactly what Madame was talking about and allowed herself to gloat. Subtle phrasing and real artistry were the very qualities the school's director had said were Leah's strong points.

"Be that as it may," Mrs. Hunter went on, "I think you just have to learn how to grab the spotlight."

Leah barely suppressed a groan. Pam was always upstaging everyone—in class, at rehearsals, during performances. After this little talk with her mom, Pam was going to be truly unbearable during tomorrow night's pas de trois. Leah willed away the picture of Pam angling to hog the curtain calls.

"And how do you suggest I go about that, Mother?" Pam asked snidely.

Mrs. Hunter seemed unfazed. "Why, take that *FootNotes* article."

Leah's back stiffened. She had a feeling she shouldn't overhear whatever Mrs. Hunter was going to say next.

"If you were pushy enough, you would have gotten that feature photo. A shot being partnered by Andrei Levintoff at this point in your life is worth all the schools and classes with Madame Preston in the world. To think that dumb-looking blond Leslie Framingham—or whatever her name is—"

"Leah Stephenson, Mother, Leah Stephenson." Pam's voice was hard and bright, and the next words out of her mouth shocked Leah. "You'd better get the name straight. She's the most gifted dancer I've seen. Everyone around here knows that. The critics already know that. I'd give my right arm to have what she has."

"Pamela," Mrs. Hunter broke in, absolutely uninterested in her daughter's feelings, "you still have it all wrong. It's not who dances best that matters in the long run. It's learning to be in the right place at the right time. Now, this Leah girl—she's not half as pretty as you. I have never cottoned to those pale, pasty types myself—but she is going to get modeling offers, and movie offers. You just wait and see. And with your looks you could have gone even further than she will someday. But you missed out, Pamela. And the only one to blame is yourself."

Leah couldn't bear to listen anymore. She crept back down the hall to the kitchen, her face flaming from Mrs. Hunter's insult. Leah had never thought much about her looks, but she felt horrified that someone should call her pale and pasty-looking.

"Hey, what's going on in there?" Kay walked in with Alex and grabbed a muffin from the table. She marched up to the coffee urn and looked Leah directly in the eye. "Is that Pam I hear?"

Leah didn't trust herself to answer. She just nodded.

"So are you going to Madame, or what?" Alex asked.

Leah shrugged and hurried back into the hall. She grabbed her jacket from the coat rack and ran out the door. She was starving, but breakfast could wait. She needed to be alone right now. Going to Madame and getting Pamela in trouble was definitely wrong, and she was afraid if she told her friends that, they'd try to talk her out of her decision.

Leah would never forgive Pamela Hunter for her tricks and lies, but she wasn't going to add to her problems by ratting on her. If Pam got kicked out of SFBA, Leah didn't want to be responsible for what the southern girl's mother would do to her.

No, Leah had to deal with Pam in her own way and in her own time. It was a private decision Leah had made, not one to be hashed out with her friends. Pam had some pretty heavy problems, and she deserved the chance to solve them.

Chapter 13

The first time Leah got to see Pam alone was that afternoon at the final dress rehearsal in the auditorium. The painters were finally gone, and though the air still smelled of turpentine, the room glowed with the fresh white paint and the newly stained antique paneling that ran halfway up the wall.

Leah was on the empty stage practicing her variation. Her gray leg warmers bunched up around her ankles as she practiced her pirouettes again and again. The tiny tiara she wore on her head changed her sense of balance, and Leah wanted to be absolutely sure when she performed today for Madame, the director would have no choice but to keep her name in the program.

"Excuse me, miss—"

Leah hopped down off pointe and looked around. A man wearing overalls grinned at her. "I've got to check the lights." He motioned toward the apron of the stage and dragged a heavy-duty extension cord across the floor. "I'll only take a minute."

Leah nodded and walked with her head down into the wings. She heard the familiar sound of someone warming up with a round of battements en cloche. It was Pam. Pam's tutu complemented Leah's perfectly, and her hair shone like copper beneath her tiny tiara. But all the makeup on Pam's face couldn't hide the fact that she'd been crying.

Leah had thought about Pam all day. She had rehearsed and rehearsed in her head the things she would say to her. But now her mind went blank. All she could hear was the sound of Pam's mother's voice and the awful ways she had put Pam down.

"Pam?" Leah took a couple of steps forward.

Pam's body stiffened, but she kept her eyes focused on the fire extinguisher in a corner by the exit door. Her battements swung up higher and her knuckles grew white. She was holding the top of the sawhorse tightly.

Leah noticed that as Pam kicked her working leg up she was throwing herself slightly off balance. Suddenly Leah had an idea.

"Last time you danced your solo, your turns were a little off. I can help you with them." Leah tried not to sound critical.

Pam's eyes narrowed to two tiny slits, and she turned slowly to Leah. "I don't believe you, Stephenson." Pam's voice was cold, and she sounded a lot like her mother. "First you go to Madame and snitch on me, then you have the nerve to tell me my pirouettes stink."

"I didn't go to Madame," Leah said simply.

"Hah!" Pam scoffed and grabbed a towel from the back of a nearby chair. She dabbed daintily at the sweat on her powdered shoulders.

"It's the truth, Pam. I decided—" Leah stopped and took a deep breath. "I decided this was between you and me—"

"And everyone else at SFBA. Come off it, Leah. I may be a second-rate dancer in the Great Stephenson's eyes, but I am not dumb!"

Leah grabbed a sweatshirt from a pile of discarded dance gear by the door and draped it over her shoulders. The tiny backstage area was drafty, and Leah's muscles were beginning to cramp.

"The other girls have promised me they won't mention any of this ever again. I swore Alex to secrecy." Leah considered her next words, wondering if they'd have any meaning to someone like Pam. "Alex never makes a promise she can't keep."

Pam looked doubtful. She stared at the floor and worked the toe of her shoe round and round in a little dent in the floorboard. "Yes," she admitted with obvious reluctance. "Sorokin is honest. It's the one good thing about her."

Leah pulled up a chair and brushed the seat off with her hand. She sat on it gingerly. "We both know what's been going on here," she said. "I know exactly what you've been up to—so do you."

A hostile glint lit Pam's eyes. "I did not try to hurt Misha," she protested.

Leah knew if she was ever to get Pam to trust her, she had to trust Pam on this point. She remembered the look of pure joy on Pam's face when she had displayed the kitten to the other girls. "I believe you," Leah said. "I really do believe you."

There was an awkward silence, and Leah didn't know what to say next. She only knew whatever she said had to be the truth, and she had to sound honest. "Pam, I know we're enemies." The word was strong, and it surprised her even as she said it.

Pam made no motion to deny it.

"And I don't want to keep being enemies. I respect you too much as a dancer."

Pam looked up quickly. "Come on—"

"I do. And I don't think we should keep fighting with each other. There's a lot I could learn from you."

Pam arched her eyebrows and looked at Leah hard.

"I mean it, Pam," Leah went on. "My jump isn't as good as yours. I haven't got enough flash and sparkle in my dance. Robson said that. You heard him."

"You can't always believe what Robson says." Pam snickered. "He wouldn't know he had another Pavlova in his class if she came neatly labeled and with a proper Russian accent."

The idea made Leah laugh, and Pam laughed, too. But before the serious mood changed, Leah quickly added, "And there's stuff I could teach you."

"Like what?" Pam challenged.

"How to turn. Your pirouettes are too violent. You rush through them too much. I think it has something to do with your preparation." Leah made that up as she spoke, but she knew she was on the right track.

Pam studied Leah a moment. "Are you saying you want to be friends?" she asked quietly, hope in her voice.

As hard as it was, Leah had to be truthful. "Uh—no. Not exactly." Leah tried to ignore the way the light went out of Pam's eyes and hurried on. "But we can respect each other and treat each other like human beings. This isn't a war, you know. It's a ballet school, and we both want to learn to dance."

Pam didn't say anything for a minute. Then she fluffed out her tutu and marched past Leah right onto the stage. The electrician and his basket of wiring paraphernalia had vanished. Pam stopped at stage center and planted her hands on her hips. "So are you going to teach me a proper pirouette, or am I going to wither away here waiting for you?" she asked.

"Alex, it's the truth, I swear it! Pam is a changed person," Leah claimed the next night as she pressed a towel against her face to soak up the sweat. She was wearing her fourth act white tutu. The final curtain on the scholarship performance of *Swan Lake* had just fallen, and it was the first chance Leah had to tell Alex about her showdown with Pam.

Dancers from the Bay Area Ballet were milling around backstage, helping the girls straighten their hair for curtain calls.

A basket of red roses stood in the wings, a present from the rest of the cast for Katrina. Katrina looked exhausted, but her translucent skin glowed pink beneath her makeup. Her performance had been incredible, and Leah had run up to her and pressed her hand before running off-stage to leave Katrina and Kevin and Michael Litvak, who had danced the role of the evil sorcerer, Van Rothbart, alone for their solo bow.

"Leopards do not change their spots," Alex insisted. "And Pamela Hunter is a girl I will never, ever, trust. I do not care how nice she acted to you today. Be careful, Leah. I will not tell you again."

Then Alex grabbed Leah's hand, and all the swans ran out onstage. The curtain went up to thunderous applause. The auditorium was small, but it seemed as if half of San Francisco had squeezed in to see the school's first full-length ballet performance of the year.

Looking very dapper in his tuxedo, Christopher Robson brought the roses onstage. He handed them to Katrina, who bowed and blushed, and then turned around and curtsied graciously to her corps. She plucked the first rose and handed it to her partner. But the second one she picked went right to Leah, and Katrina's eyes held Leah's for a second. There didn't have to be words between them: Leah had bowed gracefully to Katrina's winning the lead in the performance. The rose was Katrina's way of saying thanks.

Leah found herself wishing she had a rose to give to Pam.

The curtain fell again, and Madame glided over to Leah. "The pas de trois tonight was wonderful. I think you three should take a solo bow."

Madame beckoned Kenny toward her and then gestured into the wings. Pam ran up, her eyes sparkling. Madame looked at Pam and said quietly, "I have never seen you dance better. Mr. Robson said your pirouettes were the best you've ever done."

"I know," Pam crowed. "He told me." She sounded a little smug. She smiled at Leah. When Madame's back was turned, Pam winked at Leah as if to say it was their little secret.

Behind Leah, Alex groaned, but Leah was not going to pay attention to her. "They were wonderful, Pam," Leah commented.

"And you danced well yourself, Leah." Madame's comment was carefully understated, but her eyes shone with praise. Madame knew Leah had been through something, and she was obviously pleased that Leah had danced her way past whatever disasters had happened in the last two weeks.

Leah's heart was singing as Kenny took her by the hand and guided her and Pam toward the curtain. Someone held it open, and the three young dancers stepped through into a generous round of applause. Leah sank into a graceful bow, the exact way she had been taught, not too deep, not too showy, but expressing gratitude to her audience for accepting the gift of dance she had brought to them.

Kenny pressed her hand gently, and she straightened up. She turned and ran lightly into the wings and turned around smiling ... expecting Pam to follow her. But Pam was still up by the footlights blowing kisses to the audience. Kenny waited a moment. He was supposed to linger, to gallantly allow Pam offstage before him, the way the two had practiced their bow at the last dress rehearsal. Finally, with a disgusted look on his face, Kenny strode angrily back behind the curtain. "I don't believe that girl," he cried.

"I do," Alex said. In spite of Leah's warning glance she spoke up loud and clear. "It takes more than a little kindness and coaching to get some leopards to change their spots!"

Pam finally bounced back behind the curtain, her face open in a wide smile. "They loved me!" she cried, genuine tears streaming down her face. She hurried past Leah, past Alex, and right past a startled Madame. "They loved me," she repeated again, loud enough for everyone to hear. She pursed her lips, grabbed Leah's towel off the back of a chair, and tenderly dabbed away the tears that streaked her makeup.

Adagio—Slow tempo dance steps; essential to sustaining controlled body line. When dancing with a partner, the term refers to support of ballerina.

Allegro—Quick, lively dance step.

Arabesque—Dancer stands on one leg and extends the other leg straight back while holding the arms in graceful positions.

   Arabesque penchée—The dancer's whole body leans forward over the supporting leg. (Also referred to as *penché*.)

Assemblé—A jump in which the two feet are brought together in the air before the dancer lands on the ground in fifth position.

Attitude turns—The *attitude* is a classical position in which the working or raised leg is bent at the knee and extended to the back, as if wrapped around the dancer. An *attitude turn* is a turn performed in this position.

Ballon—Illusion of suspending in air.

Barre—The wooden bar along the wall of every ballet studio. Work at the barre makes up the first part of practice.

Battement—Throwing the leg as high as possible into the air to the front, the side, and the back. Several variations.

> *Battement en cloche*—Swinging the leg as high as possible to the back and to the front to loosen the hip joint.

Batterie—A series of movements in which the feet are beaten together.

> *Grande batterie*—Refers to steps with high elevation.
> *Petite batterie*—Steps with small elevation.

Bourrée—Small, quick steps usually done on toes. Many variations.

Brisé—A jump off one foot in which the legs are beaten together in the air.

Centre work—The main part of practice; performing steps on the floor after barre work.

Chainé—A series of short, usually fast turns on pointe by which a dancer moves across the stage.

Corps de ballet—Any and all members of the ballet who are not soloists.

Dégagé—Extension with toe pointed in preparation for a ballet step.

Developpé—The slow raising and unfolding of one leg until it is high in the air (usually done in pas de deux, or with support of barre or partner).

Echappé—A movement in which the dancer springs up from fifth position onto pointe in second position. Also a jump.

Enchaînement—A sequence of two or more steps.

Fouetté—A step in which the dancer is on one leg and uses the other leg in a sort of whipping movement to help the body turn.

Frappé (or *battement frappé*)—A barre exercise in which the dancer extends the foot of the working leg to the front, side, and back, striking the ball of the foot on the ground. Dancer then stretches the toe until it is slightly off the ground and returns the foot *sur le cou-de-pieds* (on the ankle) against the ankle of the supporting leg.

Glissade—A gliding step across the floor.

Jeté—A jump from one foot onto the other in which working leg appears to be thrown in the air.

Jeté en tournant—A jeté performed while turning.

Mazurka—A Polish national dance.

Pas de deux—Dance for two dancers. (*Pas de trois* means dance for three dancers, and so on.)

Pas de chat—Meaning "step of the cat." A light, springing movement. The dancer jumps and draws one foot up to the knee of the opposite leg, then draws up the other leg, one after the other, traveling diagonally across the stage.

Penché—Referring to an arabesque penchée.

Piqué—Direct step onto pointe without bending the knee of the working leg.

Plié—With feet and legs turned out, a movement by which the dancer bends both knees outward over the toes, leaving the heels on the ground.

> *Demi plié*—Bending the knees as far as possible leaving the heels on the floor.
> *Grand plié*—Bending knees all the way down letting the heels come off the floor (except in second position).

Pointe work—Exercises performed in pointe (toe) shoes.

Port de bras—Position of the dancer's arms.

Posé—Stepping onto pointe with a straight leg.

Positions—There are five basic positions of the feet and arms that all ballet dancers must learn.

Rétiré—Drawing the toe of one foot to the opposite knee.

Rond de jambe a terre—An exercise performed at the barre to loosen the hip joint: performed first outward (*en dehors*) and then inward (*en dedans*). The working leg is extended first to the front with the foot fully pointed and then swept around to the side and back and through first position to the front again. The movement is then reversed, starting from the fourth position back and sweeping around to the side and front. (The foot traces the shape of the letter "D" on the floor.)

Sissonne—With a slight plié, dancer springs into the air from the fifth position, and lands on one foot with a demi plié with the other leg extended to the back, front, or side. The foot of the extended leg is then closed to the supporting foot.

Tendu—Stretching or holding a certain position or movement.

Tour en l'air—A spectacular jump in which the dancer leaps directly upward and turns one, two, or three times before landing.

Here's a look at what's ahead in TEMPTATION, the seventh book in Fawcett's "Satin Slipper" series for GIRLS ONLY.

Pam walked up to Kay. "Well, have you heard the news?"

Leah was pretty sure from Pam's cocky attitude that she had just snared a big scoop about something at school.

"No, but I am sure we will now," Alex commented dryly, folding her arms across her chest.

Pamela ignored Alex and shoved the paper in Kay's face. "You'll never guess who's back in town—and *why*." Pam paused and took the time to look each girl in the eye. When she got to Leah, her glance lingered just a little longer, and Leah's heart almost stopped beating.

"We do not have all night," Alex grumbled impatiently.

"All right, but you all better prepare yourselves for what I've got to say." Pam hoisted herself up on top of Alex's desk and pulled off her black suede boots. The smug, cunning smile on her face was beginning to make Leah a little sick. "I'm surprised, Leah," Pam commented. "I thought you'd have part of my story figured out by now. It's about James—you remember your old friend, James Cummings?"

"James is back?" Leah gasped.

"In San Francisco?" Alex sounded dubious. "He wrote me a letter last week—maybe two weeks ago. He said nothing then about coming back here. Where did you get this story, Pamela?"

Unfazed by Alex's disbelief, Pam slowly unfolded her

paper, which was turned to the page of theater and dance news and reviews. She tossed the paper to Alex and continued to smirk. "I guess our darling James has come up too far in the world to tell *everything* to his old friend."

Alex buried her nose in the paper. As she read, her face darkened into a frown. But a moment later she was glowing. "Leah, it is true. James is here—"

Before Alex could finish, Pam announced, "Not just *here.* Here at the San Francisco Ballet Academy to make a movie!"

"James—in a movie?!" Kay shrieked. "That's unreal."

"Not just any movie." Alex pulled Leah down beside her on the window seat and showed her the paper. "A ballet movie with the Bay Area Ballet Company—"

"And Andrei!" Leah fell back against the wall and shook her head, pushing the paper away. "How incredible, Andrei and James in the same film."

"I thought you'd love it," Pam gloated.

"But do they say who he's dancing with?" Linda asked. "With a star like Andrei, they've got to have a major female dance lead."

Leah grabbed the paper from Alex and scanned the article again. "No, they don't. They just say 'Young, promising Joffrey Ballet apprentice and former San Francisco Ballet Academy scholarship holder James Cummings, will costar with Andrei Levintoff in a new dance film called *Temptations*, to be shot on location at the War Memorial Opera House, at the Academy—'"

"Film crews at our school?" Kay cried.

Linda dropped her knitting needles to applaud. "I wonder if any of us will be in it—you know, classroom shots!" She clasped her hands together and squirmed in her chair. "I hope so. I've always dreamed of being in a movie."

"Keep quiet—go on, Leah." Alex shook Leah's shoulder gently.

"Where was I? Oh, yes. 'The ballerina who will play the dance lead has not yet been named,' " she read, " 'although speculation centers around Bay Area Ballet's own talented Diana Chang!' " Leah dropped the newspaper and let out a loud sigh of relief. "Well, that should get Diana off *my* back!" She grinned.

"I should say so," Alex agreed. "But they say it is only a rumor—"

"A strong rumor, I would say, if it's in the *Examiner*!" Kay pointed out.

"Wait, I want to know the plot," Linda piped up. She grabbed the paper from the floor and skimmed it quickly. "It's about a young beautiful ballerina who is a student. The director of the company—who will be Andrei—falls in love with her, but she is really in love with a poor, talented but struggling young male dancer."

"*James!*" The other girls all shouted in unison and burst out laughing.

"Diana is going to love it!" Pam said gleefully. "Her two favorite partners fighting over her on the silver screen!"

"But it does not say Diana will be the dancer," Alex reminded them. "I do not think if it were so sure they would say it is—what is the word?" She cast Leah a helpless look.

"Speculation."

"Yes, perhaps it will be someone else. Maybe someone the newspapers do not know about yet," Alex said, a dreamy smile crossing her face.

"Well, whoever they choose, she has to be young enough to look like a student but dance as well as Diana!" Pam observed. "And I know only one other person around here who will fill the bill."

"Who?" Kay asked eagerly. "Someone else in the company?"

"No, silly—little ol' me!" Pam announced, tossing her auburn hair over her shoulder. "I mean, isn't it obvious?"

ABOUT THE AUTHOR

Elizabeth Bernard has had a lifelong passion for dance. Her interest and background in ballet is wide and various and has led to many friendships and acquaintances in the ballet and dance world. Through these connections she has had the opportunity to witness firsthand a behind-the-scenes world of dance seldom seen by nondancers. She is familiar with the stuff of ballet life: the artistry, the dedication, the fierce competition, the heartaches, the pains, and the disappointments. She is the author of over a dozen books for young adults, including titles in the bestselling COUPLES series, published by Scholastic, and the SISTERS series, published by Fawcett.